Changeling Press. LLC

ChangelingPress.com

Bullet/Knox Duet
A Bones MC Romance
Marteeka Karland

Bullet/Knox Duet
A Bones MC Romance
Marteeka Karland

ISBN: 978-1-60521-929-5

Publisher:
Changeling Press LLC
315 N. Centre St.
Martinsburg, WV 25404
ChangelingPress.com

Printed in the U.S.A.

Editor: Jean Cooper
Cover Artist: Marteeka Karland

The individual stories in this anthology have been previously released in E-Book format.

Table of Contents

Bullet (Grim Road MC 3)
A Bones MC Romance
Marteeka Karland

Cecilia: The enigmatic biker is the one bright spot in my life. I see him three or four times a week at the cafe down the block. Talking to him about books we're reading or our hopes and dreams helps me escape my reality, if only for a short time. Most of the time we don't even sit at the same table. He's everything I ever wanted but know I can never have. We simply cross paths. Him going... wherever he goes. Me... I know I'm going straight to hell. Nothing but a miracle can save me. The Devil owns my soul.

Bullet: There's something about the small, dark-haired woman I see at the corner cafe. She's everything I'm attracted to in a woman, but she's so young it's laughable. I didn't set out to seduce her, but the next thing I know she's in my bed and I spend the most incredible night with her. I wake up the next morning to a cool pillow. No note. No way to contact her. I chalk it up to a young woman not wanting drama in her life until I see her again a few days later. This time, she's in my ICU, beaten to within an inch of her life. Someone's going to pay. God have mercy on their soul. Because I won't.

Chapter One

Bullet

"Just another glorious day in the ICU, Attie." The fresh-faced resident was trying way too hard to socialize. I'd noticed the pup did the same with all the attendings. I accepted he was trying to fit in and carve his place with people who would be his peers once he'd finished his residency, but no one -- *fucking no one* -- called me "Attie."

"My name," I said, not looking up from the laptop where I was finishing up a physical assessment for the patient I'd just seen, "is Atticus. Or Dr. Benedict. Call me Attie again, I'll personally see to it you fail this rotation." If the kid had been a prospect, I'd have beat the shit outta him. But I couldn't do that. Not in this world. Which was a Goddamned shame because if an adult hadn't learned how to treat people with respect by this guy's age, he needed an ass whoopin'.

I was beginning to think it was past time I left practice in the civilian world and stayed at the Grim Road compound full time. Traveling back and forth was risky anyway. The last thing I wanted was someone following me to the compound. They wouldn't be able to get in, but it would draw attention to us, which I did not want. Still. Here I was. Trying not to punch an intern.

Fuck. Me.

I didn't give the kid time to respond. Instead, I shut the laptop, picked it up, and headed back down the hall to the lounge. I wanted to finish my day so I could get a bite to eat -- and maybe some stimulating conversation that didn't involve body fluids or death. I'd had enough of that in the Air Force. I'd thought I'd fulfill some sense of purpose by continuing to work with critically ill patients in a different setting, but death was death.

"He's just trying to fit in, Atticus." One of my colleagues, Phil Davis, clapped me on the shoulder as he pulled up a chair. "Don't be so hard on the kid."

"I've told him repeatedly not to shorten my name. I'm tired of fuckin' with him."

"He'll make a decent doctor if you help train him right."

"I'm not a mentor, Phil. I told you that when you hired me. I'm supposed to be an intensivist. Not a teacher." It was a sore spot. The hospital had promised me I wouldn't have to supervise interns or residents. Yet here I was.

"You know how it is, man. There's a shortage of healthcare staff. That includes doctors. Why keep these kinds of hours when you can do family medicine?" He shrugged. "The hospital owns the offices, so they all get paid a salary just like we do. Only difference is the hours. They get nights, weekends, and holidays off. We don't."

"Coulda had better pay and better benefits if I'd stayed in the fuckin' Air Force," I grumbled. "Kid's got this last chance. He calls me Attie again, I'll do more than fail his rotation. I'll kick his fuckin' ass."

Phil chuckled, likely thinking I was joking. I wasn't. "Just give me report so you can get your cranky ass outta here. Someone needs a beer. And possibly to get laid."

I scowled at him, but he was right. On both counts.

Report took an hour. We walked around to each of my ten patients' rooms, and I gave him a rundown of what was happening as well as introduced him to each of those patients. Not every doctor in the hospital wanted to do hand-off rounds like this, but I thought it helped all of us to see the patients as people instead of simply numbers on a screen. As such, I insisted on it.

We only got caught up in one room and honestly, Mrs. Singleton loved to talk.

"I thought I was taking the right dose, Dr. Benedict. I mean, I might have missed my shot from time to time, but I usually manage better than this." She smiled up at me from her bed. She was always pleasant. And always called me Dr. Benedict. "Maybe if you explain it to me again?" She looked like she was hoping we'd sit down and go over her medication with her again, but didn't want to actually say so.

"Maybe we should get you an insulin pump," Phil said, not looking up from his tablet as he pretended to review her chart. I knew he was just giving himself an excuse not to engage. Mrs. Singleton had been offered the same thing every single time she was admitted. She always refused. Something Phil knew all too well.

"Oh, I couldn't. It might give me too much. What would I do then?"

"It won't give you too much, Nanny." Phil's irritation showed on his face and in his voice, but he never looked up from his fucking tablet. "It's programmed to give the exact amount we order. You need to agree to this so you don't have to be admitted so much. You're going to ruin your kidneys and your eyesight, among other things."

"I'm ninety-two, Dr. Davis. If my kidneys and my eyesight were going to go, they'd have done so already. Besides, I know I'm not long for this world." She sounded like she was going to cry. It made me want to beat the shit outta my colleague.

"You don't have to do anything you don't want to," I said, sitting beside the bed and taking Mrs. Singleton's hand. One thing I tried to always do was be respectful to my patients. Just because she was old didn't mean she was stupid. "We've discussed this before. If you want to keep taking shots instead of using an insulin pump, you can. But he's right that you're hurting your body. I'd like to have long conversations with you for years to come." I gave her a gentle smile.

She patted my hand with her free one. "You're a good man, Dr. Benedict." Then she sighed, looking resigned. "If you think it's best, I'll agree to your pump. Do you promise it will be OK?"

"I do, ma'am. I'll even come check on you after you're released until you get used to it."

Her eyes grew wide. "You'd do that? For me?"

I smiled. "You're one of my favorite patients, Mrs. Singleton. Of course, I will."

Mrs. Singleton was a diabetic who went into ketoacidosis once every couple of months because she didn't take her insulin correctly and refused to modify her diet. At ninety-two years young, I figured if she wanted to eat cupcakes and moon pies, that was her prerogative. My job wasn't to judge but to help her when she got sick. I'd often wondered if she didn't do this to herself on purpose to get some attention because her daughter and grandson refused to put her in a nursing home but were never around to take care of her. She'd been a social butterfly in her younger years, by all accounts, and needed personal interaction. But she abided by her family's wishes and stayed at home even if her daughter and grandson were never there to help her.

After we left and started down the hall, Phil

chuckled, as if he hadn't insulted and treated the elderly woman horribly. "I swear, that woman gets chattier every time we have her." He shook his head. "I don't have time to spend thirty minutes in her room chatting about the weather or the good old days. Not to mention arguing with her about her treatment."

Yeah. It was past time I either opened my own practice or simply moved back to the clubhouse and disappeared from polite society.

I gave Phil a hard look. "You know, if you had half as much sympathy for Mrs. Singleton as you do that disrespectful punk of an intern, you might be a decent doctor."

I left Phil alone with Intern Iggy and the rest of the zoo and headed out. I needed the sun on my face and the wind in my hair. Fuck this shit. I'd keep my promise to Mrs. Singleton no matter what, but my days here were numbered.

Coming back into the doctor's lounge, I went to the locker room and changed out of my scrubs and lab coat. I left very little at the hospital other than a couple changes of clothes for emergencies, so packing my stuff wouldn't be an issue. Tomorrow I'd bring my truck and clean out my shit. Tonight, however, I was on my bike. I wasn't prepared.

I strode out of the hospital, my boots thudding on the pavement as I made my way toward my sleek black Harley V-Rod. The bike that would carry me away from the sterile walls and white coats. I needed the freedom of the road and the comfort of my club. Grim Road MC had been good to me. After my last mission it had become my only real haven. Initially, working at the hospital had fulfilled my need to help people, but it had become more cumbersome than helpful now.

Flashes of the carnage I'd lived through shot through my brain and I gritted my teeth through the pain, needing to keep myself under control. It was those memories that haunted me at night and kept me coming back to the hospital to work. I hadn't been able to help the people from that day so long ago, but I could help people in the here and now.

I started up my bike, put it in gear, and took off. I needed food and rest. Tomorrow everything would be better. I'd get Mrs. Singleton to stick to her promise to try the insulin pump. God knew Phil would just fuck things up. Besides, I wanted to help her get home so I'd know where to come to check on her and make sure she was using her pump correctly. I also needed to put the fear of God into her daughter and grandson. I was pretty sure they were trying to keep her out of a nursing home so they could keep her Social Security check and that simply wasn't going to happen.

With a sigh, I pulled into the parking area of a little outside café I often frequented after work. Helped me to wind down and catch my breath. Occasionally I'd run into someone who knew me, but the hospital was in Palm Beach so it wasn't often. It was also the place where I'd met the most interesting woman I'd ever encountered.

Her name was Cecilia, but she went by CeCe. I thought she was an escort, but the jury was still out. She was here nearly every evening. I found I simply liked talking to her. She was intelligent, with a quirky personality. She could carry on a conversation about almost anything with some degree of knowledge. But it was her eyes that intrigued me. She had the look of someone who'd seen far more than a person of her years should have. I doubt she was much out of her teens, but she seemed to take in everything around her.

Several times I'd tested her. Dropping observations about things around us or small details about someone walking down the sidewalk. She always knew the answers. Like me, she always chose a table that let her have the best view of the area with her back against the building.

Walking to my usual table, I glanced around, looking for CeCe. Because of the long conversation with Mrs. Singleton, I was a little late so I could have missed her. I hoped not because I could really use her refreshing personality. The girl really was a rare treasure. I thought about prying into her life, finding out exactly what she did and who she worked for, seeing if my suspicions were correct, but we had a comfortable relationship. Basically, we spoke when we were at this café, and that was it. I didn't see her anywhere else. We didn't talk about anything personal. Sometimes we never even looked at each other. Just… talked. About everything and nothing. Nonsense. Whatever was on our minds. I was about to leave when I saw her.

CeCe was dressed in a tight, short red skirt with a white billowy top that cinched around her middle above her waist. A black bustier pushed her breasts up and together, giving her mouth-watering cleavage. Her hair was a straight, gleaming mass dark as a raven's wing, reaching below her waist. This was her usual attire and I'd learned a couple of months ago to live with the hard-on I got seeing her in these outfits.

She sat along the brick wall of the building beside the café, as usual, one table between us. We didn't acknowledge each other or speak. She simply caught the attention of Teddy. He owned the place and was always there, even if he had someone else working.

"The usual, Teddy."

"Chocolate pie and a coffee coming up, darlin'."

"Thanks." Everything inside me settled. I hid my smile and said nothing. Instead, I picked up a book I'd been reading the last several days while I drank a cup of coffee and ate a sandwich. This evening it was chicken salad.

"You still reading about the guy who kills that old lady and then spends the whole book freaking out about it? Raskolnikov, right?"

I grinned. "*Crime and Punishment*. Yeah, kid." I didn't look up from my book, but I never did. It was a game we played, where we pretended indifference. It was one we were both comfortable with. "I always found him to be an interesting character -- tormented by his own guilt. Unable to escape the consequences of his actions."

She snorted. "It's always something, I guess. Life torments us all in one way or another."

I thought about that. "Can't say you're wrong there."

"'Course, I'm not wrong." She sounded bitter. Not for the first time, I wondered if I was right and she was an escort. She was always very well put together. Even the revealing clothing she wore was done with taste. Her hair was always perfect, her makeup just so. Her body was well toned, fine muscle playing beneath her skin when she moved. I'd never seen such perfectly formed arms on a woman before. They were muscled but sleek. Feminine.

With a last quick bite of pie, she slapped a couple bills down on the table and stood. She started to leave, then stopped and turned her head to face me. "You think Raskolnikov would've done any better if he'd had someone? You know, someone who had his back?"

"Who knows?" I shrugged. A darkness crept into her gaze even though her face was carefully blank. This, I didn't like. "But I do believe there are times when the ends justify the means. Maybe not in Raskolnikov's case, but…"

"Yeah." She looked away, putting her shoulders back. "Sure."

"See you tomorrow?" I'd never pushed her before. Never asked when I'd see her or if she'd be back. But my instinct was screaming at me that something was wrong.

She shrugged. "Don't know. Maybe."

"Take it easy, CeCe." I forced myself to let it go even though I wanted to push even harder, to make her tell me what was going on and how I could help. Because if ever there was a woman who needed help, it was CeCe.

"You too, Atticus."

CeCe had *never* called me Attie. She left without a backward glance. I wanted to follow her. Knew I should. Something seemed just that little bit off, and I had the feeling she was in trouble. Her body language belied her flippant attitude. I glanced at the table. She'd barely nibbled at her pie, which wasn't like her. The love affair she had with refined sugar and chocolate was, at times, nearly orgasmic. She savored every single bite.

Yeah. Something was definitely off.

"Kid's gonna get hurt one day." Teddy picked up her plate with the pie she'd picked at and shook his head sadly. He was in his early sixties and had run the café as long as I'd been in Riviera Beach. He stayed out of people's business, never prying or even making much small talk, but he noticed things.

"You know where she works?"

"Works." He scoffed. "You know as well as I do she's a hooker. High-end, but she still answers to a pimp."

"You know who?" I knew I was asking more than I should. The last thing I wanted was anyone knowing how much this girl had piqued my interest. I worked outside of Grim Road, but I was still a club member. Very few women I knew could handle club life.

Our new vice president, Lemon, might be making some fundamental changes, but Rocket was still easing her into everything we did. Some of it -- some of the things I'd done for my country and my club -- were straight out of Hollywood. Most of it was either classified top secret or black ops, not on the books at all. *Some* things would probably earn me life in prison after that administration was out of office. If I was lucky.

When I told CeCe sometimes the ends justified the means in reference to *Crime and Punishment*, I hadn't been speaking metaphorically. I'd killed, but never without a reason I believed justified the killing.

He shrugged. "Word on the street is Ettore Alfonso. He stays on the down low, but I heard he's mafia. Italian."

Yeah, I'd heard of Ettore Alfonso. He ran operations on the eastern seaboard in the south, most of it through the Port of Palm Beach. He got his girls to America from various countries through the cruise ships frequenting the port, as well as fencing stolen goods out of the US. The Italian mafia had been relatively quiet since Gotti had been imprisoned, but that was mainly a front. The current boss was keeping things off the radar as much as possible. Alfonso was nothing if not cunning.

"She don't need to be in that life."

"Ain't my business, but I don't disagree."

"Do me a favor, Teddy."

"Yeah?"

"Put anything she orders on my tab from now on. OK?"

"You got it. Someone needs to take care of that girl."

I nodded my agreement. "I'll do what I can." Which meant, I needed to get Crush and Byte on this. I wanted to know anything and everything I could about Cecilia Reyes.

Chapter Two

Cecilia

It took everything I had to not throw something, or release a primal scream. *What a fucking day. What a motherfucking day*!

Ettore was sending me to an associate he needed something from. I had no idea what and didn't much care. The less I knew the better in most cases. But this guy was a fucking pig. Every time he needed Marco's assistance, instead of money the man asked for me. Which meant, once I got to Marco's, I'd be there at least a week. Every fucking second of it disgusting and degrading.

I had an hour before I had to be there and I needed to calm down or I'd end up worse than humiliated and fucked. Marco could get rough. More than rough. But as long as Ettore got what he wanted, he didn't care. I was nothing but a piece of flesh to him. Apparently a very expensive piece of flesh since I knew for a fact Marco didn't get money from his assistance. He got me. The only condition Ettore gave him for his use of my body was that I not be scarred or permanently injured. Marco always pushed it close to the limit. I knew in my heart he'd obliterate that line one day. And there wasn't a Goddamned motherfucking thing I could do about it.

As was my habit before a job, I went to the outdoor café run by a guy named Teddy. The man was hard working and loved the little café he owned. I'd heard him telling people more than once it had always been a dream of his wife's to own something like the little restaurant. It was hard work, and he always seemed to be operating very close to the red, but it made him feel closer to her. His only regret was that he hadn't gotten it up and running before she died.

My heels clacked on the sidewalk as I approached. Unerringly, my eyes went to the set of tables he'd set up for the café along the brick wall out back. The building served as a boundary for the café. It also afforded me a place I could sit and not have to worry about someone sneaking up on me from behind. There was very little I could do if Marco came looking for me or sent one of his goons after me, but I wanted to see it coming so I could prepare myself.

Sure enough, there was my rock. Atticus Benedict.

I'd started coming to the café for the chocolate pie. Kept coming back because Atticus was usually there. I knew he was more than he seemed. I'd heard he was a doctor in Palm Beach over at JFK North. If that was true, he didn't act like a doctor. He was certainly smart enough, I suppose. He didn't look like a doctor. Which was stupid thinking. I didn't look like a hooker, either.

Or maybe I did. I was pretty sure Teddy saw through me. If that were true, then Atticus definitely knew. Which made me all the more angry, because I didn't want him to see me that way. Anyone else? I'd tell them to go fuck themselves. But Atticus was the kind of man I dreamed about, but knew I'd never attain. At least, not in any meaningful way.

I made my way to my usual table. Thank God no one had claimed it, though there were several people enjoying Teddy's food this evening. Before I could signal to Teddy, he was there with a piece of the chocolate pie I loved so much and a cup of coffee.

"Thanks, Teddy." My voice was tight, but soft.

"Kinda crowded in here this evening." Atticus didn't look up from the puzzle he was working in a little magazine. Like one of those grocery store puzzle books old people in nursing homes did to keep their minds occupied. Why not use his phone? There were plenty of games to be played there.

"What the fuck are you doing with *that*?" I put as much disdain in my voice as I could. Was I spoiling for a fight? How would pissing off Atticus, the one man in this whole fucking city I could count on for good conversation to take my mind off my life for a few minutes, be of benefit to me? Was I trying to drive him away?

Maybe.

He glanced up at me. There was no surprise on his face, in fact, if anything, he looked slightly amused. "It's called a crossword puzzle."

"Wouldn't it be easier to do one on your phone? Might save a few trees."

He snorted a laugh. "Might." He pointed to the chair across from him, but I shook my head. I needed to have my back to the wall. Surprisingly, he scooted his chair around, putting himself more at an angle with the wall and the open sidewalk and gestured to the space he'd vacated.

Unexpectedly, I felt a wave of something like grief envelop me and I found myself near tears. These two men, men who knew very little about me, were treating me with more kindness and respect than anyone had in my entire life. Especially since I'd been brought over from Italy. My childhood hadn't been great, but it had been better than my life in America.

Still, I hesitated. "I don't want to interrupt."

"You're not." Atticus again gestured to the empty space beside him.

With only a slight hesitation -- more for show than anything else -- I picked up my pie and coffee and set them on his table before moving a chair around to sit with my back against the wall.

"Rough day?" Atticus asked with a raised eyebrow and a knowing look.

"Gonna be," I muttered. "How about you?" We never asked about things like this. Personal things.

He shrugged. "Not bad. Convinced someone my advice was good advice. I'm hopeful this person's health will improve, but I'll still drop in to check from time to time." He didn't elaborate and I didn't question further. I'd only asked because he had.

Knowing I probably needed to offer something in return, I fiddled with my pie. I desperately wanted to eat the rich dessert, but I wasn't sure my stomach could take it. Or the coffee. "I have a job." I cleared my throat. Damned thing was trying to close up on me. Emotions sucked. "I don't want to do it, but..." I shrugged. "It's like everything in life. Sometimes you gotta do what you gotta do."

Atticus nodded. "Sometimes. Maybe."

"Always." I knew I sounded bitter and the conversation was turning heavy. The last thing I wanted was for him to bail on me. "So." I gave him what I hoped was a cheerful smile. "You always read about murder for personal gain, or do you do light reading?"

He grinned, just like I'd hoped he would. "I read everything from technical journals to crime novels. Not much I won't try at least once."

I wrinkled my nose. "Technical journals? You mean, like medical stuff?" When his expression shifted slightly, I hastily added. "I heard you're a doctor or something. Don't worry. I'm not gonna ask for free medical advice or anything."

"You can ask me for anything you want, CeCe.

Medical advice or anything else."

I gave him a wry smile. "Don't mean you'll give it to me, though. Right?"

He held my gaze with a steady one of his own. "I didn't say that."

"You didn't have to." I gave him a cheery smile. "Besides, I said I wasn't gonna ask." Before he could say something to make me cry, I changed the subject. "Wow. The breeze is really nice today."

He nodded, his expression not changing. He seemed to study me, like he was looking for something in particular. "It is. Supposed to be bringing a bit of bad weather."

"Yeah, I heard there was something coming in. Not a hurricane or anything."

"No. Weather could still be dangerous, though. You got a good, solid place to stay?"

Was it my imagination or was there a double meaning to his words? "Good as any, I guess."

"I got a spare bedroom if you need to crash." I shook my head and opened my mouth to speak, but he cut me off with a raised hand. "No strings, CeCe. Just a sturdy, dry place to stay, maybe some dinner, and good conversation."

God, if only!

"I --" I swallowed. I wanted that. So fucking much! But if I didn't show up at Marco's, Ettore would kill me.

Or worse.

"I can keep you safe. From everything."

My insides fluttered even as disappointment was so strong one tear managed to leak from my eye before I could stop it. Tears were a weakness I couldn't afford to show. Not in front of anyone. But especially not Atticus. That feeling he was something more than what he appeared to be was stronger than ever as I searched his face for... something. Deliverance, maybe? My whole life I'd belonged to Ettore Alfonso. From the time I was born in Italy to now. He'd made it abundantly clear I'd always belong to him.

But what if I could have my own life? What if I were free to do whatever I wanted to do? Be with whomever I wanted to be with? Undoubtedly, I'd want to be with Atticus. More than one night, too. If he was the man I thought he was. And really, how many men sat here night after night talking to someone like me, knowing what I was, and never hit on me?

"You and I both know what I am, Atticus."

"Sure. You're an intelligent, beautiful young woman."

"I'm a whore," I said softly. "Have been for a long time."

"You can be anything you want to be, Cecilia."

"Right. I hear you." He had no idea how wrong he was. I still flashed him a cocky grin. "Maybe today I'll be one of those sophisticated bitches in Manalapan. I'll crook my finger and everyone will do my bidding."

He grinned at me. "I absolutely believe you could get everyone around you to do your bidding."

Before the conversation could continue, my phone buzzed. Ettore. I shivered, knowing I was already late. I should have been at Marco's ten minutes ago. I was surprised either man had let it go this long before reaching out to find out where the fuck I was.

"You gonna answer that?" Atticus raised an eyebrow and nodded toward my phone.

"Spam," I muttered, sending the call to voicemail and shoving it into my handbag. I took a deep breath. "You know what? Maybe I'll take you up on your offer. Be spontaneous. Right?"

"Yeah." His drawl was sexy as shit. Even though he'd said there were no strings, I wasn't certain I wanted it that way. What would it be like to have sex with someone of my own choosing? That was something I'd never experienced. God knew, if I could pick someone for sex, it would be Atticus. "Spontaneity can be fun."

"If you were serious about that offer?" I really hoped he wasn't fucking with me.

"Absolutely serious, CeCe. No strings. No expectations."

I took a bite of my pie. The only bite I'd managed so far. Decision made, my stomach settled. I'd deal with tomorrow. If this was my last night on Earth, I was going to enjoy myself to the fullest.

Chapter Three

Bullet

Christ, I had to be careful. Underneath all the bluster and the shroud of indifference she draped over herself, CeCe was a woman hurting. I knew from experience in medicine she likely equated her worth with her sexuality. I counted it a win she was willing to take shelter with me from the storm that was supposed to hit later tonight. It meant that, on some level, she trusted me. Trust was the first step in getting her out of the bad situation I suspected she was in.

I paid the bill -- she protested when I paid for her pie, but Teddy overruled her, saying her money was no good to him when she had a perfectly good man willing to pay -- and took her to my bike.

"Wow," she breathed. "Nice ride." For the first time since I'd met CeCe, the smile on her face was genuine. No shadows. No guarding her reaction.

"You can ride with me or, if you have your own ride, I can give you directions and you can meet me."

"No. Sometimes I take the bus, but usually I walk. It helps clear my head."

I grinned. "And work off the sugar buzz?"

"Most definitely the sugar."

She hiked up her short skirt and climbed on the bike, as I held out my hand to help her. "Be mindful of the pipes, honey. Don't burn yourself."

"Well, if I do, will I get that free medical advice I said I didn't want?"

"Honey, you can have anything at all you want. All you have to do is ask." She sucked in a breath before shaking her head slightly and climbing on behind me. I ignored her sudden discomfort and reached for her arms. Wrapping them around my waist, I said, "Hang on. Now that you made it on without burning yourself, I don't want you falling off the back."

"You sure you're not just trying to get me to feel you up?"

"Never said that."

"Fine. But if I accidentally brush my fingers over your dick, I don't want to hear any complaints."

I glanced over my shoulder and gave her a smirk. "Honey, you touch my dick, I guarantee you there will be no complaints whatsoever."

Her laughter was the sweetest music. She actually sounded happy. Was there any better sound? Yeah. I was fucking fucked. Shit was, I wasn't broken up about it. What I *was* concerned about was coaxing her to stay with me. Not just tonight, but... for a while. Because if she went back to Ettore Alfonso, I couldn't keep her safe from the bastard. While I was confident I could satisfy her intellectually, I had to be careful about her feeling like she didn't have choices. I absolutely wouldn't take her from one life with no choices to another.

But I was getting ahead of myself. And I wasn't sure what I'd do if she wanted to stay anyway. I couldn't take her back to the club. At least, not right away. Not only would she likely freak out -- going from a mafia kingpin to an outlaw biker wasn't exactly what I'd call a step up in the world -- but I'd need to get permission from Rocket. Or Lemon. I grinned. Yeah. I could get Lemon to agree to let CeCe in the club for protection whether or not I made her mine. Which wasn't likely.

"Want to take a walk on the beach first?" I asked the question spontaneously. I hadn't really planned to do anything other than get her home, comfortable, and maybe get her to drink a little alcohol so she'd sleep. I absolutely wanted to do everything I could to get her to stay with me.

"A walk on the beach?"

I looked back over my shoulder. "Yeah. You know. Watch the sunset and shit."

Again, she laughed. "You don't seem like the type to like long walks on the beach to watch the sunset."

"I'm not. Just thought it might be something a woman would appreciate."

"I would appreciate it. Just wasn't expecting you to suggest it."

On impulse, I took her hand from around my waist and kissed the backs of her fingers briefly. "We can pretend it's a first date. And I never allow a woman to get handsy on a first date."

That really got a laugh from her. She actually put her hands on her cheeks before wiping tears from her eyes before she wrapped her arms around my middle once more.

"Yeah, Atticus. I think that would be beautiful. I mean, since we're not getting handsy anyway."

"Exactly." I patted her hands once before starting my bike and taking off.

Never had I experienced anything like that fucking ride to the beach. And yeah, I took the long way. There was still about an hour before sunset. The sky hadn't started to turn colors yet so I knew we had time. Because CeCe was… Well, if she wasn't having the time of her life, she was having some kind of psychotic break. The girl whooped and hollered, like she was on a rollercoaster ride at an amusement park. At one point, she wrapped her arms around my waist and rubbed her face against my back like a kitten.

In the back of my mind, I knew we should both be wearing helmets, that eye gear at the very least was required by law, and neither of us had either. It wasn't the smartest thing I'd ever done, but getting her to come with me, getting her out of a situation she obviously didn't want to be in and giving her the chance to be somewhere safe, was worth the risk. I just had to be careful and get us to our destination safely.

When the sky began to darken with streaks of purple and red, I pulled off next to a secluded section of beach close to my house. It wasn't very big and was too close to the highway to be much of a destination for people to stay very long, but at night it was one of the most beautiful places in the city.

I pulled my bike under the pier and killed the engine. "Careful of the pipes."

"You told me that once. I think I can remember." Despite the words, CeCe didn't sound annoyed at all. I still held out my hand to help steady her as she climbed off from behind me.

"Just takin' care of my girl."

"Your girl, huh?"

"Well, yeah. This is a first date. Right?"

Her tinkling laughter filled me with more satisfaction than I'd ever felt before. Not from grateful patients I'd helped, not from my brothers in arms. Not even from my MC brothers. This woman's simple laughter as we bantered and flirted did something to me that I knew I'd never feel again outside her presence. I still wasn't prepared to commit myself to taking her for my own, but I knew one night in her presence would never be enough.

As I climbed off my bike, CeCe took off her heels, sinking her bare feet into the sand. She groaned. "God, that feels good!"

"The warm sand on your feet?"

"Yes. I hadn't even realized how my feet ached." She smiled up at me, her hair blowing gently in the breeze.

I smiled down at her and brushed strands of her hair behind her ear. "Then let's get you out there where the sand's warmer. See if we can't ease that ache."

We stared at each other for several long moments. I swear, I've never wanted to kiss a woman so much in my fucking life. I brushed my thumb along her bottom lip and she gasped slightly, parting her lips. I thought she was going to take my thumb into her mouth, and I knew I'd lose my shit if she did. Instead, she gave me a serene smile like she didn't have a care in the world. Somehow, that look was better than if she'd offered to suck my thumb. Or my cock. In the weeks since we'd started talking, I'd never seen such a look of contentment on her face and was determined to keep that look there.

I cleared my throat. "Come on." Taking her hand, I led her from under the pier out onto the beach. The sky was streaked with bright red and purple. The sun was at our back as we looked out over the ocean so there was an unobstructed view of such beauty, I had to wonder if God himself was smiling on what I was doing.

"So beautiful," she whispered as she gazed out at the sea. "The sky reflects on the water and makes the water pink. Isn't that crazy?"

"I agree. Very beautiful." I didn't mean the sky. Or the water. Her gleaming hair reflected the light as she moved, giving her an ethereal look. Like an angel with a little bite to her.

We sat in the warm sand and watched the sky

and birds flying overhead. She slipped her arm through mine and leaned her head on my shoulder, never saying a word. I heard her phone buzzing several times in her purse, but she ignored it so I did too.

As it grew dark and the wind started to pick up, I leaned over and placed a kiss on top of her head. "Come on, honey. Let's get back to my house before it starts raining."

"How far is it?"

I shrugged. "A block. Right around the corner."

Soon after, I pulled my bike into the garage and shut it down. I steadied CeCe as she dismounted, then followed her, shutting the garage door and opening the inner door to the house.

Once inside, after I'd locked the door, CeCe stepped close to me and wrapped her arms around my neck. My hands automatically went to her hips.

"Atticus..." Her breathy whisper brushed over my mouth just before her lips met mine. And any thought I had of keeping her at arm's length, of keeping this nonsexual, went out the fucking window.

Her kisses were more tentative than I'd have thought, but I didn't care. The fact that she was kissing me at all was more than I should have allowed if I wanted to win her trust, but by God and Holy Christ, it felt fucking *good*! She rubbed against me, welcoming my tongue when I thrust it between her lips. I couldn't help it! The second she offered, my body decided it was doing whatever the fuck it wanted to, and it fucking wanted to do CeCe. In the Biblical sense. I had to get a fucking grip, or this was going to get way the fuck outta hand. And it was already way the fuck outta hand.

With more willpower than I ever knew I

possessed, I pulled back and rested my forehead against hers. My breaths were ragged, like I'd been running forever without a break. I was pretty sure I'd broken out in a sweat, and I was trembling like a fucking schoolboy looking at a porno for the first time.

"Sweet, God, CeCe. You're fucking delicious."

"Please don't stop." Her whispered plea was nearly my undoing. But, fuck me! How could I take what she offered and still prove to her I wasn't like everyone else in her life? I wasn't one of her johns. I wanted like anything to fuck her until she passed out with pleasure, but not until she understood this wasn't just a passing fancy for me.

"Baby, I don't want to, but I promised you this wasn't about sex. First date, remember?"

"Please, Atticus." Her voice broke on my name. "Please."

"Baby…"

She put her fingers over my lips to silence me, never taking her forehead from mine. "I've never had sex with a man because I wanted to. I've never enjoyed sex. I've never really wanted to have sex." She removed her fingers and pressed her lips to mine again before continuing. "I want to now. With you. Can you show me what it's really like?"

"I've got shit in my past I'm not proud of, Cecilia. If you live the life I think you do, then you're around men like me every fuckin' day. And I'm not talkin' about the men they send you to." I didn't spell it out. If she wanted to acknowledge she was in Ettore Alfonso's stable, I'd listen, but I wasn't going to embarrass her or in any way lead her to believe I was trying to control her or nose into her life. "But I've never taken advantage of a woman. I've paid women for sex but only if it was what we both wanted and did my fuckin' best to make sure she enjoyed herself as much as I did. So, as much as it pains me to tell you this, I can't fuck you. Not and look at myself in the mirror later."

"This isn't a transaction, Atticus. I don't want this for you to pay me, or even in repayment for taking my mind off shit every time we see each other at the café. This is something I need." She kissed my chin, then my mouth again. When she rubbed her cheek against mine, I felt the dampness of her tears where our skin touched above the edge of my beard. "I don't want to beg, but I will if I have to."

"I can only take so much, honey. Be really sure this is what you want. Really fuckin' sure. I'm tryin' to do the right thing, but I ain't no saint."

"I'm sure. Just one night, Atticus. Give me one night and I promise I'll never ask again." The lost note in her voice, the desperation to feel... *something*, was clear. Cecilia knew what she wanted and was going after it.

"God help us both, Cecilia." I barely got the words out before I pulled her into a tight embrace, then found her lips again.

Her arms tightened around my neck and she followed my lead, kissing me back as desperately as I kissed her. The more we kissed, the longer this intimate embrace went on, the hungrier I was for her. She must have felt the same way because it wasn't long before she was clawing at my shirt, trying with everything she had to get it off me.

I snagged the back between my shoulder blades and whipped the thing off before threading my fingers through her hair and continuing to kiss her. With wicked thrusts of my tongue, I tasted her, tangled with her own delicate tongue as I tried to take my fill.

The tremors running through her body were as real as the fire in my veins. She moaned into my mouth, a sweet and desperate sound that made me harden even more. I couldn't remember the last time I felt this way, but it was all I could do to keep my hands from tearing off her clothes and worshiping her like she deserved.

My cock was hard as a motherfucker. There was no way she didn't feel me pressed against her belly even through our clothes. Cecilia rubbed against me like a cat in heat. Unlike most women I'd been with, she wasn't covered in heavy perfume. No. The scent she was currently rubbing all over me was her own sweet fragrance.

She was such a contradiction of sin and innocence it was hard to keep my wits about me. On one hand, I was sure she could take whatever I dished out physically, but I knew without a doubt she would struggle emotionally. Well. She'd said she wanted to enjoy this, to have sex with a man of her choosing. Even though I knew it wasn't the best idea, I was going to give her what she wanted. I was also going to make it as pleasurable for her as I possibly could, no matter what I had to do to achieve that goal.

With a little whimper, CeCe pulled her skirt above her hips and shimmied out of her panties. She still had her heels on from the bike ride here and the thought of fucking her in those heels was a fucking turn-on. But that was not the way this was going to go. Neither was me fucking her while we were both still dressed.

"Come here," I said, pulling her closer and lifting her before she could respond. She gasped, hugging my waist with her thighs as I carried her to my bedroom.

The moon had risen to a bright, full ball in the

sky, shining through the window to my bedroom and bathing the bed in a silvery light. Like a spotlight shining on an altar of sin, ready for the virgin sacrifice. CeCe might not be a virgin in the strictest sense, but I was willing to bet my left nut this experience would be a first for her. A man intent on her pleasure. And, yeah. That'd be me.

I set her down beside the bed, urging her to strip completely. She trembled where she touched me, but it didn't take much coaxing before she stood naked in front of me. I picked her up again and laid her gently on the bed before moving back to take off her shoes.

She looked up at me, eyes wide, sweat glistening over her perfect, perfect body. She had no tattoos or piercings which I thought unusual, but was glad of it. While some were beautiful, I knew firsthand the damage that could be done with any kind of piercing if someone was sadistic enough.

"This goes only as far as you want it to, honey. This is about your pleasure. What you want." I shook my head. "I absolutely will not hurt you or in any way force you to do anything you don't want. You understand me?"

"But I --"

"No buts, CeCe. I'm gonna eat you 'til you come. Several times if I can. If that's enough for you, that's all we do."

"Atticus?"

"I'm serious." I scooted her farther onto the bed, blanketing her small form with my much bigger one. Her pussy mashed against my bare belly. My jeans were still on and I had no intention of taking them off unless she insisted. "If I can give you what you need without fuckin' you, that's what I'm gonna do. Tell me you understand." That last part was an order, pure and simple.

Her eyes widened and she gasped. Her nipples puckered and she immediately clapped her hands over them and squeezed. "Holy shit," she whispered.

I narrowed my gaze and tilted my head in confusion. "What's wrong? I need to dial it back," I muttered.

"No! No, please. I-I just never thought..." She swallowed and shook her head slightly. "That tone of voice. It's never been sexy. You know. Before."

"So I do need to rein it in."

"Not at all! I liked it. From you."

The grin splitting my face had to be positively wicked. "I think I can work with that."

I lowered my face to her chest, urging her to move her hands to give me access. I caught a nipple with my tongue, taking one long swipe over the puckered nub. CeCe let out a low moan, arching her back. When I latched on to her nipple, she cried out and shuddered beneath me.

I played with her other nipple, tweaking and pinching lightly with my fingers before switching to that peak with my mouth and sucking gently.

"A-Atticus..." Her shuddering, ragged voice hit me hard. Like a punch. I glanced up at her, needing to know she was good and I wasn't triggering something negative inside her. She looked down at me with shock, her eyes glassy, her lips parted.

"Talk to me, CeCe. Tell me what you're feeling." I released her just long enough to talk before laving her nipple with the flat of my tongue.

"G-good... s-so g-good!" She seemed unable to catch her breath. Her fingers bunched and tugged at my hair, but not like she was trying to pull me away from her. It was more like she needed something to ground her which I was more than happy to provide.

"Do you want more?" My voice was rough. I scraped my beard over her nipple, back and forth, causing her to cry out again.

"Yes! Please!"

"Tell me what you want, pretty girl. Tell me what to do."

"My pussy," she gasped.

"It's a beautiful pussy. But what about it?"

She gave a little frustrated whimper. "Touch it."

I slid my hand down past her waist to where her mound had pressed against my abdomen. She was bare and so fucking soft and smooth. I wanted to fasten my mouth over her and just fucking feast, but it wasn't time for that yet. Instead, I dragged one finger back and forth through her folds, grazing her clit occasionally. Every time I did, she jerked and cried out like she'd never been touched like this before when I knew she had.

"Oh, God!"

"Talk to me, Cecilia." I wanted to use her full name. I got the feeling everyone called her CeCe and I wanted to be different. I wanted the whole experience to be different. "Tell me what you like. What you need. Tell me, and it's yours."

"Put your mouth on me." Her voice was so soft I almost didn't hear her.

I looked up, meeting her gaze and holding it for several seconds. "You want me to eat this beautiful pussy?" I sucked her nipple between my lips again and gave a strong suck, flicking the bud with my tongue.

"Yes, Atticus. So fucking much!"

With a growl, I tore my lips away from her breast, my eyes flaring with lust and hunger I had no hope of disguising. She was wet, ready for me, and I wanted to take her that very second. Wanted to fuck her until I took us both to oblivion. But if I could bring her pleasure, if I could show her that sex could be fun and joyful and all the things women like to read in fantasies and romance novels, then I'd take care of myself later. Likely to visions of Cecilia writhing on my bed on the verge of madness as I pleasured her to infinity and beyond.

"Fuck, Atticus, please," she begged when I hovered over her pussy, my mouth a breath from her flesh. Her hips rose to meet my fingers where I continued to stroke and tease. Her breathing was ragged, her face flushed. I could see her eyes glazing over, and I knew she was close.

Never looking away from her beautiful face, I lowered my mouth to her pussy and swiped my tongue through her wet folds.

"That's it, baby. Let go," I whispered to her, trying to coax her into embracing everything she was feeling. To just… come.

When I closed my lips around her clit and sucked while fluttering it with my tongue, Cecilia exploded in a wet rush. She screamed, her fists tightening in my hair as she ground her hips, rubbing her cunt firmly over my face where she needed it most.

I'd been around the block a time or two. I've had more women than I wanted to think about. Most had a good time. Ain't saying I satisfied every woman I'd ever been with, but if I didn't it wasn't for lack of trying.

This woman, however, made me feel like a fucking king. She made love with abandon, embracing the pleasure I gave her and reached for more. I knew it was purely instinctual on her part because no prostitute, no woman whose job it was to make a man feel good, ever let herself go like this.

Cecilia shuddered beneath me, her body trembling in aftershocks of pleasure. I could feel the heat washing over me, but I refused to let myself get swept away just yet.

"You all right?" I asked, my voice hoarse with need.

She nodded, her eyes glazed over with pleasure and shock. "I-I think so?"

I barked out a laugh. "You think so?"

"Yeah. I'm not really sure."

"What can I do to make you sure?" I let my beard rub over her bare mound as I looked up at her. I kissed the skin just below her navel before nipping it slightly with my teeth.

She sucked in a breath, her eyes going wide. "Do that again," she whispered.

I did. This time, I laved the skin I'd abused with my tongue before delving my tongue into her belly button. She whimpered, her skin breaking out in goose flesh, her nipples drawing impossibly tighter.

"Talk to me." I rubbed my chin back and forth. I knew my beard was precariously close to her clit but not quite hitting it. I knew because her hips bucked spastically while she continued to whimper. Her chest and face were flushed and she still had this adorably dazed look on her face.

"Will you... do that again? Eat my pussy?"

I grinned. "Ain't nothin' in this world I want more, baby."

Chapter Four

Cecilia

I didn't even want to think about how many men I'd had sex with in the past. Never, with all those men, had one of them ever gone down on me. There were a few who'd touched me, but mostly it was a fuck-me-from-behind kind of thing where they got their jollies, or else they had me suck them off. Most of the time, it was in degrading ways that made me want to vomit.

It wasn't for me to question. I went where Ettore told me to go. He didn't send me to a man with stipulations on what he could or could not do to me, or have me do to him. He wasn't allowed to kill me and that was pretty much it.

This whole thing with Atticus? I didn't know what to do with the sensations. I wouldn't say I'd never had an orgasm before, but if I did, it was an accident and likely early on in my... service to Ettore. And never like this. Masturbation? Yeah. No. I could honestly say this was the first time I'd actually enjoyed sex.

I lay there, Atticus still lapping at my pussy, and I couldn't form a coherent thought, let alone put into words my gratitude for what he'd given me. I knew I wanted more, wanted to experience everything this man could give me.

"Please, Atticus... I-I need you..."

"You need more, baby?" He lapped at my clit again, and I shuddered. With a gasp, I tried to close my legs.

"Sensitive?"

"Y-yes!"

"Mmm..." He moved down to lick my pussy, thrusting two fingers inside me and finding a spot deep inside me that set off yet another orgasm, this one sudden and breathtaking. I literally could not catch my breath as my whole body seized.

I screamed. And screamed. And screamed. Until I was sobbing, begging him to fuck me, to put me out of my misery. To never let this stop.

The next thing I knew, Atticus was over me, his body in the cradle of mine. My legs wrapped around his hips and I could feel his cock through his jeans. Still the man would not take off his fucking pants!

I reached between us to unbutton his pants, but he stopped me, putting my hands above my head and lacing his fingers through them. Tears streaked from my eyes down my temples as I pleaded with him to fuck me. I wasn't even really aware of what I was saying.

Atticus kissed me gently, rubbing his beard over my cheek and neck. He kissed my jaw and whispered in my ear, praising me, trying to bring me down but I didn't want to come down.

"God, Atticus! Fucking please!"

"No, baby. I'm not gonna fuck you. I told you that's not happening." His body quaked and I reveled in his weight pressing me into the mattress.

"But I need it!"

"I know, baby. I know. I'm sorry." He continued to kiss me, then he rocked his hips and the pleasure started again. "Ride it out. I'll take care of you, honey. I swear it."

With those words, I rocked my hips, moving with him to put the friction on my clit that I desperately needed. A few seconds later, one last explosive orgasm rushed through me. I screamed, gripping Atticus as tightly as I could until the wave passed.

When it did, I finally ran out of energy and a lazy, exhausted lethargy settled over me. Atticus let go of my hands and rolled us over so that he was on his back with me draped over his side. He kept saying soothing things, but my brain had shut down along with my body.

As Atticus continued to whisper to me, I started to drift. For the first time in longer than I could remember, I welcomed sleep, knowing that as long as I was with Atticus Benedict, I was safe. No one could hurt me. No one could force me to do anything I didn't want to. I thought Atticus was saying something similar to me, reaffirming my own thoughts.

I knew there would be hell to pay later with Ettore and Marco, but right now I was with Atticus. His voice was so soothing, his body warm and wrapped around me like a protective cocoon. I took one last, deep breath before surrendering to sleep and the embrace of Atticus Benedict.

* * *

Bullet

My balls fucking ached. I'd fallen asleep with the most passionate, beautiful woman I'd ever met. I'd pleasured her until she'd begged me to fuck her and I had held back as much as I could. I'd promised her from the beginning I wouldn't fuck her and I hadn't. She'd thrown one over on me when she'd kissed me the second we'd walked into the house, though. I went a lot further than I'd intended to, but I'd done my level best to pleasure her as much as I was capable.

As I slowly came awake, becoming aware of more than just my blue balls and morning wood, I realized I no longer had a warm woman in my arms.

I reached over to the other side of the bed. The

pillow and sheets were cool and I groaned. CeCe had been gone for a while.

"Fuck." I lay back with a *thud*, beating myself up for being all kinds of stupid. I'd likely scared her off. I'd known I needed to go gently with her, to help her realize I didn't bring her here for the use of her body.

The first rays of sunlight pierced through the curtains, casting a warm glow that failed to chase away the chill creeping into my heart.

"CeCe?" I called out, my voice thick with sleep and worry, as I sat up in bed. The echoes of our passionate night still clung to my skin, but the absence of her presence made it all feel like some cruel fantasy.

Silence greeted me, its mocking whispers tightening around my chest like a steel band. A cold sweat broke out on my forehead as I threw off the sheets and stumbled out of bed, a heavy dread sitting in the pit of my stomach.

"Damn it," I muttered, pulling on my jeans and scanning the room for any signs of her departure. "She's done a fuckin' Houdini."

I moved through the house, my heart pounding in my ears, hoping against hope that she'd simply wandered off to explore or take in the ocean view. But as I flung open the front door, the bitter taste of disappointment settled on my tongue. She was gone, vanished without a trace, leaving nothing behind but the ghost of her touch.

"Son of a bitch," I growled, slamming my fist against the doorframe. Pain jarred up my arm, but I welcomed it. "You really did a fuckin' number on me, didn't you, little CeCe?"

More than my desire for her, a stronger need to keep her safe rose to the fore and threatened to consume me. Everything in me wanted to go hunting.

But I couldn't. I knew I couldn't keep a kitten who didn't want to be kept. I'd see her again. When I did, we'd get a few things fucking straight.

Like how she was never in the fuck going back to Ettore Alfonso, even if it meant I had to raze the entire Italian mafia on the lower Eastern seaboard.

Chapter Five

Bullet

Mrs. Singleton was supposed to be released today if they got her pump ready and she was comfortable using it. I had made it my personal mission today to do what I had to in order for the elderly woman to be comfortable with her treatment. She deserved to have the best care I could give her, but my attention to Mrs. Singleton wasn't purely selfless. I was trying to distract myself from the fact that I hadn't seen CeCe in seven days.

I worked seven on, seven off. The night I'd spent with CeCe had been the end of my last day on shift. In the following days, I'd gone to the Goddamned café every fucking night, and no CeCe. She might have missed one or two days, but not more. Not unless she was avoiding me. While that was certainly possible, I didn't think she'd completely ghost me. If for no other reason than she loved that fucking chocolate pie.

As I walked into the dictation room, I picked up my tablet, checking the status of Mrs. Singleton's insulin pump. I wanted to speak with her before she left and reassure her I'd be by to check on her every day.

"You've only got three to sign off on, Atticus." Dr. Mason was in his late fifties or early sixties. He was very much old school in that he liked to get to know his patients. He was one of the most intelligent clinical doctors I'd ever had the pleasure of working with. "Two will be going home. You already know Mrs. Singleton. By the way…" He grinned at me as we passed the room of the woman in question. "Thank you for convincing her to get the insulin pump. I hope you intend to follow through with your promises to her." Yeah, the other man was calling me out, making sure I wasn't just blowing smoke up the old woman's ass.

"I do." I shrugged. "I'll have all the time in the world when I turn in my resignation."

That caught the other man by surprise. "Atticus? Surely you're not leaving. We need you here."

"I can't anymore, John. This whole place has been one fuckup after another."

"I know they put some residents and interns under you, but it won't be for long."

"I'm not a teacher. I'm a soldier. Always have been."

"Well, if you're half as good a soldier as you are a doctor, the hospital could still use more of you. Not less."

"Like I said. I'm not a teacher."

"Yes, you are. You taught Phil not to be such an ass. He actually apologized to Mrs. Singleton the day after you called him out." Dr. Mason chuckled. "He also tightened conduct for his interns and residents. So, you see? We need you."

"I appreciate that, John. But my rare spots of joy are overshadowed by frustration. I have some things to finish, then I'm not renewing my contract."

"Well, as long as I'm here, you'll have an ally if you want to come back." He took my arm and guided me toward a room to give me report on the last patient I'd receive from him before he went off shift.

"This is a sad case." John took off his glasses and pulled a handkerchief then began polishing the lenses. He shook his head slightly as if that would negate what he was about to tell me. I could tell from the tight expression on his face whatever he was about to tell me would be bad. Also, that itching sensation between my shoulders got worse and I almost reached back to scratch it. "This young woman was found in an alley five nights ago, beaten and raped. She's been in and out of consciousness for a couple of days now. This morning's been the first she's been awake more than a few minutes at a time, so everything up to this point has been under Jane Doe. I think they're working to get that fixed but you know how it goes. It'll take a few hours to get it all straightened out. We can sit down in the dictation room and I'll go over it all with you before I leave."

I glanced at the chart on my tablet. "Mother fuck…" This couldn't be right. I stepped into the room, tossing the tablet on the counter by the sink and crossed to the bed where a small woman lay battered and bruised. Her arms were covered in finger marks and there were several scrapes and small cuts. Her face had been beaten so badly it was hard to recognize her, but when she opened her eyes and looked up at me…

"Atticus?"

"Yeah, honey. It's me." I sat on the bed next to her, taking her hand in mine and bringing it to my lips. "I'm here."

"You know her, Dr. Benedict?"

Fuck. How could I have completely forgotten Dr. Mason was there?

"Yeah. Cecilia Reyes."

"Do you want to pass her case to someone else?"

"Absolutely not." My response was immediate and probably too vehement given how CeCe flinched, but there was no way in hell I was letting anyone else take care of CeCe as long as I had privileges at this fucking hospital. "She's under my care and will be until she's ready to go home. You make sure everyone knows that."

"You won't be here twenty-four/seven, Atticus."

"For her, I will."

He raised his hands. "I'm on the next six nights, Atticus. If you need me, I'll be happy to look after your girl while you're off shift."

CeCe whimpered, her gaze clinging to mine even as she tightened her hand around mine weakly.

"I've got her. I'll take care of her."

"I understand." He gripped my shoulder. "Keep her safe, Bullet."

That got my attention, and I turned my head sharply to give him a hard look. "How do you know that name?"

He tapped his finger to his temple. "Ask Crush and Byte."

"Oh, I will." I gave him a death stare. I liked John, but I wouldn't hesitate to kill him if he was a threat to the club.

"Got my own secrets, Bullet. I just want you to know, I'll do my best to keep the heat off you if necessary." There was a wealth of meaning in that declaration. "If you need anything, call me."

What the fuck? I made myself a mental note to discuss this with Crush and Byte at the first opportunity…

I stilled. Yeah. I needed to get Grim Road involved with this sooner rather than later. Why? Because what Rocket knew, Lemon knew. If she thought I was trying to keep secrets, especially ones involving someone vulnerable, she'd have my balls and I wouldn't blame her.

CeCe had closed her eyes again. I glanced at the monitor to confirm her vitals were stable and her heart was in the right rhythm, then pulled out my phone and called Lemon.

"Wassup, Doc?"

I winced. Yeah. I really shouldn't get mad at Intern Iggy when my vice president was just as bad.

"I need club help. I have a woman I need to bring there to disappear."

"What do you need?" It was a demand more than a question. Lemon was now all business. The VP of Grim Road.

This surprised me. I knew Lemon was protective of the women and kids in the compound, but I had no idea how that would translate to someone she didn't know. Instead of asking a lot of questions before making a decision, or deferring to Rocket, Lemon simply demanded to know what I needed.

"She needs to disappear, Lemon. Then I need to go hunting."

"How many men do you want ready?" Again, no questions asked about why. Just what did I need.

"I'll discuss it with Rocket. I'll need his help planning because this could have some serious blowback, so I'll defer to him."

"I'll have Rocket call church. Can you get details to Crush discreetly so we can make a game plan?" Which was code for can I do it in a way that couldn't be traced back to me or to the club. Thankfully, Crush and Byte already had that system in place. It was the first thing they'd done when Lemon took over as VP after the incident with Hammer and Claw.

"Tell him I'll text him what I have."

"What does *she* need, Bullet? What do I need to have ready to make her comfortable?"

God, this woman was the perfect vice president. I know a few of the guys were leery or even outright objected when Bear had first brought us the idea to make Lemon vice president, but I knew without a doubt it had been the right choice. The more time passed, the more I knew I'd been right. Bear had been right.

"A comfortable room with enough space I can have some hospital equipment brought in. Can you get her some clothes too? Loose-fitting stuff."

"I'll have it by the afternoon. What do you need to get her home?"

"Tell Knox I'll call him. I'll need something easy for her to get in and out of. Might need the RV so she can lie down."

"We'll get it ready. You bring her home, and we'll take care of her."

"Thanks, Lemon."

"We're family, Bullet. We take care of our own."

As I ended the call, I shook my head. I honestly wasn't sure that I got what Lemon had been talking about until this very moment. I was Air Force. I'd had brothers in arms and we were very close for a while. I hadn't had that relationship with anyone since right before I'd been recruited by the CIA. After that, I learned the less said the better. To protect CeCe, I'd take all the help I could get.

"Why'd he call you Bullet?" CeCe's words were slurred, and she could only open one eye. Probably the pain meds. She was on a pain pump, which I'd have to transition. No way I was doing the kind of paperwork it would take to get that thing and the meds out of this hospital. Once we left here, she was going to disappear off the face of the fucking Earth.

"It's my road name, honey. Long story, but we'll have all the time in the world to talk about it. Just not now. Right now, I need to get you ready to move."

"Where'm I goin'?"

"Home with me. My real home with all my

family. They're all gonna protect you, and I'm going to kill the son of a bitch who did this to you."

Chapter Six

Cecilia

My world was foggy and disjointed. I thought Atticus had told me he was going to kill someone, but that couldn't be right. I hadn't seen Atticus since I'd left him after that one night. I think the pain in my heart was worse than the pain from the beating I'd gotten later.

I was sure I'd wake up with Marco or one of Ettore's capos standing over me. No. Not a capo. I wasn't that important. It would be one of his soldiers ready to pick up where Marco had left off. The only question was, how long would this go on before they let me die?

"Yeah. I have everything ready. She's not ready to leave yet, but I don't think we have a choice."

I wasn't sure who was speaking, but I thought it sounded like Atticus. But that was crazy. I knew it wasn't Ettore. He'd never take the time to come to the hospital over a whore. Marco either. Like he gave a shit. Ettore finally let him do what he wanted to me and it had been everything I'd expected. My only surprise was that I wasn't dead. Yet. Likely an oversight on his part.

The conversation continued, but it was one-sided. Was someone talking on the phone? "No. I can take care of her at the compound. I can get everything I need other than narcotics. She had a small brain bleed, but the CT they took this morning just came back. It's improved and she doesn't seem to have any motor or speech deficits other than what was caused by the pain medicine. Kid's a fuckin' lightweight, but that's actually a good thing. Means it will be easier to keep her pain under control until it's manageable." Another pause. "Yeah. Be here in an hour. I'll have everything ready by then."

"Who's there?" I tried not to sound like a scared kid, but my vision was still kind of blurry and I couldn't tell who was in the room with me. It sounded like Atticus, but I couldn't tell for sure.

"Hey, honey." The voice that had been so hard-sounding a few moments ago was now soft and friendly. The bed beside me dipped and he took my hand in his. I thought he brushed his lips over the backs of my fingers, but I wasn't sure. "It's me. Atticus."

"Bullet."

There was a silence before he spoke again. "You remember that?"

"The doctor from before called you that. You said it was your road name." I was struggling not to slur my words, to clear my head when it felt like it was stuffed full of cotton. "Are you..." My breath caught in my throat. If he was part of the mafia too, I wasn't sure I'd survive this. Ettore likely thought I was dead, which meant if I could manage to get out of here without him knowing I was alive I might be able to leave Florida and go live a normal, quiet life under a different name somewhere the mafia didn't give a shit about. "Are you in a gang or something?"

"No, honey. Well, I'm part of an MC, which you're going to find out about shortly."

"A m-motorcycle club?" I knew my voice was basically a whimper, but I couldn't keep the dread and sheer terror out of my voice.

"Shhh... baby. Just relax. I swear it's not what you're thinking."

"I can't go back to that life... I can't do..."

He leaned down and brushed his lips over my

forehead. "You won't. I swear it on my life. All you need to do is rest and I'll take care of everything."

"If he finds out I'm still alive, he'll want me back." I thought I felt a slight burn in the bend of my left elbow and turned my head. There was an IV tube running there hooked to a pump that was whirring softly. "What's 'at?" Yeah, things were starting to close in on me. Everything sounded like it was echoing in the room around me, and my ears were ringing.

"Your last dose of pain meds before I get you out of here."

"Where're we goin'?" I needed to focus, but it was an impossible task. I could feel myself fading fast.

"I'm gonna keep you safe, Cecilia. That's all you need to worry about."

"Please don' hur' me."

"Never, baby. I'll protect you with my Goddamned life." He brushed his lips over my eyes, making me close them, so very gentle despite his harsh words and the growl to his voice. "Let the meds take you. I'll take care of everything else."

* * *

The next time I was aware of anything, I was in a different room. This place didn't smell like a hospital. Instead, there was the soft fragrance of lavender and eucalyptus, with a fresh ocean breeze wafting over my face. I was in a comfortable bed with lots of pillows and a light comforter draped over me to my waist. I was in a man's oversize T-shirt and -- oh, my God, it smelled like I remember Atticus smelling.

"Far as we can tell, Ettore Alfonso isn't looking for her. I seriously doubt he cares if she's dead. But if he finds out she's alive, he'll definitely send a soldier after her."

There was a small whimper somewhere close to

me. I knew the feeling. The thought of Ettore finding me made me wish Marco had finished the job he'd started.

The side of the bed dipped and a warm, rough hand enveloped mine. "Hey there, baby." Gentle fingers brushed a lock of hair from my forehead. "Pain meds wearing off?"

I blinked my eyes open, focusing on the man sitting beside me. Atticus looked worn out but determined, his gaze unwavering as he assessed me. "You're safe, CeCe. I won't let anyone hurt you," he said, his voice low and soothing. "You know that. Right?"

I struggled to sit up, wincing at the sharp pain in my side. I clamped a hand over the spot but hissed in a breath when that hurt too.

"Easy." He gently removed my hand before moving to help me sit, fluffing pillows behind my back and head. When he was satisfied, he sat back on the edge of the bed. That's when I noticed a big comfortable-looking chair sitting beside the bed. There was a trash can beside it loaded with what looked like crushed Red Bull cans.

"How long I been out?"

He shrugged. "A day. Bettin' you need the bathroom."

I tried to roll my eyes at him, but not only did it hurt, I just couldn't commit. If he was right and I truly was safe, then I was willing to bet he'd done a metric shit ton to make it so. "Now that you mention it."

"I'd ask if you wanted a bedpan but I'm pretty sure I know the answer to that. Besides, I'm not a nurse. But I will carry you to the bathroom."

"No." I spoke quietly, a little embarrassed to need help at all. "But I'd appreciate it if you helped me so I don't fall. Not sure I could take the pain if I did."

"Absolutely."

He stood and waited patiently for me to decide to push the comforter back. I thought I knew I was wearing panties and a shirt, but nothing else. I took a deep breath, blood rushing to my face as I flushed in embarrassment.

"You know what?" I cleared my throat because it was trying to close up and I was close to tears. "I'll be fine on my own." I swiped at my eyes when a couple of tears, the motherfuckers, overflowed.

Atticus opened his mouth when there was a soft knock at the door followed immediately by a small woman entering the room. She had on jeans, motorcycle boots, and a leather vest over a black T-shirt. She was young. Maybe late teens or early twenties. What was crazy was, when she'd first entered the room, with a welcoming smile on her face, she actually looked the part of a carefree young woman. The second she saw my tears, her expression had changed, transforming her face completely to something like, "Fuck with me at your own peril."

"Bullet? What the fuck'd'you do ta her?" She rushed over to me, shoving Atticus out of the way.

"Bullet," I mumbled. "Guess I need to get used to that."

She tilted her head. "Get used to it? What do *you* call him?" She seemed genuinely curious.

I started to answer, then glanced at Atticus. He shrugged so I spoke. "Atticus. Um, he's a doctor."

The woman nodded. "Yeah. I got he's a doctor. Haven't decided completely if I like him or not, though he's got some great fruit punch. Didn't know his name was Atticus. Sounds very... patrician. Stuffy." She turned to Atticus and narrowed her eyes. Something passed between the two and I got the feeling Atticus was bracing himself for whatever came next. "Maybe I'll shorten it to --"

"You will not shorten it." Atticus cut her off and actually growled at her. "You'll fuckin' call me Bullet." If he'd directed that look and tone of voice at me, I'd have run from him, screaming. Or, considering how sore I was, waddled carefully to the bathroom and locked the door.

This woman just tilted her head thoughtfully. "Attie got an Attie-tude?"

The giggle that escaped my throat was unbidden but unavoidable. Attie-tude. That was just too damned amusing.

"See? She thinks I'm funny."

"That's 'cause she don't know you yet." Atticus nodded in my direction. "Cecilia, this is Lemon. Lemon, Cecilia."

"Call me CeCe." It was automatic. Something I told everyone. I didn't really mean it, though. It was something I used to separate CeCe from Cecilia.

Lemon studied me for several seconds before shaking her head slowly. "No. I think Cecilia is who you are." She smiled. "Come on. I'll help you to the bathroom. This Neanderthal can go clean up and find us something to eat. That way you can get on top of the pain before it overwhelms you."

"Pretty sure I'm the doctor, Lemon."

"Pretty sure I'm the vice president, Bullet."

Lemon gently helped me to my feet and let me lean on her until I got my legs under me. I hadn't been on my feet since I got to the hospital. The other doctor said I hadn't been conscious at all the first three days I'd been there. After that I was in and out. Inactivity combined with the pain meds they'd had me on made me weak as a newborn kitten.

Surprisingly, Atticus didn't argue with Lemon. Though he wasn't really the kind of person to argue much. I thought he was more the type to give a person a hard stare that promised retribution so bad that person would immediately apologize and never commit the infraction again.

"I'll be back with food," he said. "I promise I'm not leaving."

"It's fine," I said. Again, it was automatic, when all I really wanted to do was beg him not to leave me. I thought this Lemon might be all right, but I didn't know her. And I wanted Atticus.

"No. It's not fine. But Lemon's right. I'll get you some food, then you need some painkillers. You don't need to take them on an empty stomach." He held my gaze. "I won't be long, Cecilia. I'll be right back."

I nodded. I needed to go to the bathroom, but I was afraid to let Atticus out of my sight for some stupid reason. "You… you promise?"

"I swear it, honey. I'll not leave you without telling you where I'm going."

"Ouch." I winced. "Guess I deserved that."

Lemon looked from me to Atticus. "Bullet…"

He raised his hands. "That's between Cecilia and me." He brought his focus back to me. "Which we'll be talking about. Later."

"I'm so sorry," I whispered.

"No need to be sorry. Just promise it won't happen again. We talk to each other from this point forward."

I felt like a naughty child, but I nodded. "I promise."

He gave me a satisfied smile. "Good. Now, let Lemon help you with your business. Take a shower if you feel up to it. There's a hairbrush and toothbrush in there for you. I think Lemon and Apple brought clothes for you earlier. You can put on a fresh shirt, but make sure it's not tight. Loose-fitting clothing until you've finished healing."

"Are you always so bossy?" The question slipped out before I could censor it. I blamed it on the lingering fuzziness from the pain meds.

Lemon barked out a laugh. "Yeah. The bastard is always that bossy. You get used to it. Then you bust his balls." She shrugged. "I only had to do it once. He's a fast learner. Well, fast compared to the other Neanderthals in this club." She urged me into the bathroom as she continued talking. "Wait until you meet Falcon. Ask him about his bike. He loves to talk about his bike."

I got the feeling that was a setup, but I didn't think it was to get me in trouble or make me look foolish. No. This was a woman who was solidly in my corner. If she wasn't, she wouldn't have cared if she called me CeCe or Cecilia.

Lemon helped me undress, wrapping me in a towel before helping me with my shirt. I was able to get my underwear off and still keep the towel on and not expose myself.

The other woman chatted lightly while she set the water in the shower for me. There was a bench along one end. She'd placed the shampoo, conditioner, and shower gel within easy reach.

"You good if I leave the room? I'll stay if you feel dizzy or too weak to do it yourself." She looked at the floor, toeing a rug. "I didn't want help, but I needed it. When I got hurt."

"You?" Fear hit me like a punch to the gut and my legs gave way. Thank God Lemon was close by or

I'd have hit the floor. "They hurt you?"

"What?"

"The m-men h-here."

"Oh, hell no!" Lemon looked like I'd presented her with the head of a unicorn. "No one in this club would dare. We had a guy who did. He didn't last long." She stopped, then shrugged. "OK, so he did last a long time. Way the fuck longer than he wanted to last, but that's not the point. The point is, no one in this club would ever allow you to be hurt by another member of this club. Anyone tries, you come to me. I'll take care of it. But, honestly, after Hammer, even if there was anyone left who was capable of hurting a woman like that, they wouldn't. It was that bad. No. I got hurt when some guys thought I was Venus."

"If that's supposed to make me feel better, it's really not." It kind of did, but I didn't really want to say so.

She smirked. "Is too."

"Yeah. Maybe. Who's Venus?"

"She's from Salvation's Bane. Piston claimed her and she let him, but it's been kinda rocky goin' for 'em. Not 'cause he's mean or anything. Venus is testing him. And fuck if she's not having a great time doing it. Not that she'd admit it. You'll meet her later." She studied me for a moment. "You think you're up to a shower? If not, you can just wash pits and pussy. Worry about an actual shower later."

I couldn't help but laugh. This woman was too much. "Yeah. I think I want a shower. I feel gross."

"No offense, but you kinda look gross."

"Gee, thanks."

"Any time! Now. You need help?"

"No. I think I can manage." She turned to go, but I stopped her. "Lemon?"

"Yeah, Cecilia?"

"Thank you."

She nodded her head and gave me a grin. "Any time. You and me and Apple are going to be besties."

I wasn't so sure about that, but far be it from me to stand in the way of whatever this woman wanted. I'd give it a shot.

Chapter Seven

Bullet

Control. I had to keep control. Now that Cecilia was here and Lemon was looking out for her, I wanted with everything in my being to go hunting for that fuck Ettore Alfonso.

I stomped into the kitchen, needing to find something light she could keep on her stomach. She hadn't had solid food since she'd been at the hospital. I knew taking her out had been a risk, but the greater risk was Alfonso sending someone to check on her. Of him trying to take her again. I could manage her medical care here if I kept a close eye on her. It was mostly done but the healing anyway. She was still in pain, but that would fade. I just needed to ease her back into things now.

Soup was easy to fix. Dump a can in a bowl and pop it in the microwave. It wasn't great, but it would be easy for her to digest and, more importantly, not puke back up. I reached for the door to the cupboard but a hand on my shoulder stopped me.

"Surely you're not feeding your woman something out of a can." Apple, Lemon's twin, smiled up at me. She'd come to stay with us after leaving Iron Tzars. I still didn't know why. She hadn't even told Lemon, which likely meant she wasn't ready for anyone to die yet.

"Just looking for something easy on her stomach but filling, so I can give her some pain meds."

"Come with me." Apple led me to a Crock-Pot on the other side of the kitchen, snagging a bowl from the cabinet as she went. She lifted the lid and a wonderful smell reached me. Not too rich, but appetizing. Inside was a creamy-looking soup. Apple took a spoon and stirred it a couple of times, bringing to the top chunks of what looked like... potatoes?

"What is it?"

"My sister's potato soup. It has some herbs and stuff. Potatoes, of course. Cheese. Milk and chicken bouillon. It's kind of bland but still has flavor. Just not too much. Danica always made this for us after we'd been sick. You know. When we felt like eating. It'll get you going." She hesitated, looking off as if unsure of herself. "I thought Cecilia might need some building up."

"Lots of carbs," I muttered. "Would give her energy and strength without being too hard on her stomach or the rest of her digestive system."

"You can take her a bowl if you think it would help. Maybe some crackers to go with it?"

I gave the young woman a gentle smile. "I think that will do nicely." She flashed me a beautiful smile so reminiscent of her twin's, it was hard to reconcile the sweetness of this woman with Lemon's tartness. "Apple?" I had a question I wanted to know the answer to. I told myself it was because I wanted to look after all the women's health -- mental and physical. The last thing we needed was one of them getting overwhelmed and frightened.

"Yeah?"

"What happened to make you want to come to Grim Road? Did someone hurt you?"

Immediately, her open friendly expression shut down in such a perfect imitation of her sister's it nearly took my breath away. "No." She didn't hesitate even a second, obviously having no intention of admitting anything was wrong. Just like her sister.

"I didn't mean to intrude, Apple."

"You're not." Her welcoming demeanor didn't

return. If anything, she grew pale. Hard somehow. Whatever had driven her to Grim Road had done a number on her. "You're welcome to as much of the soup as you need. I'll come back in a couple of hours and put it in the fridge for later. She can have as much as she needs. I'll be happy to make more if she wants." She nodded once before turning and leaving the kitchen without a backward glance.

Why did our women seem to come to us just as broken and hurting as we all were?

I shook my head, then set about making a tray for Cecilia. In addition to the soup, I added some saltine and sweet crackers, as well as a glass of milk and bottles of water and Gatorade. She could have milk with the soup if she wanted. If not, there was something for her to pick from. Either way, she needed as much fluid as she could comfortably drink. I put everything on a tray and carried it to my room. The second she felt up to it, I was moving us into one of the houses in the family section of the compound. I wanted her to have privacy. I also didn't want any mistakes. If a club whore hadn't gotten the message and hurt her feelings, I wasn't sure how I'd react.

I reached our room, and I could hear Lemon chatting lightly. To announce my presence so I didn't startle them, I balanced the tray on one hand and knocked lightly. The chatter didn't stop. Instead, Lemon's voice grew louder. Seconds later, she opened the door with a bright smile. The lines around her eyes and mouth told a different story.

"Good! You brought food." She immediately took the tray from me and shut the door in my face.

"Lemon!" I growled and opened the door, stepping inside and closing it behind me.

"My bad," she called, not looking over her

shoulder. "Forgot you were there." Lemon liked dicking with us. I thought sometimes it was a defense mechanism when she wanted to avoid meaningful conversation. Or to hide her worries. The woman was brash and as sharp-tongued as they came, but she had as tender a heart as ever I'd seen.

"Of course, you did," I grumbled but eased my way farther into the room. Cecilia was on the bed in one of my shirts instead of one Lemon and Apple had procured for her. It was embarrassing how much I loved seeing her in my clothes.

Cecilia looked up at me. She picked at the bedding nervously. "I'm sorry." Her eyes started to tear up, but she swallowed them back. "I liked the way your shirts smelled. Lemon dug me one out of your dresser."

"Honey, don't be sorry about that. You can have any of my shirts you want."

"Are you sure you don't mind?" I hated that she looked so unsure and afraid. I wanted her to be the confident, assertive woman I'd grown to know over the past few weeks.

"Not at all. In fact, I might have to insist on it. Especially while you continue to heal."

She gave a relieved breath and glanced at Lemon. The other woman winked at her.

"I've got to go see Apple. You have my number for when Crush gets you a phone. If you need me before then, send a prospect or come get me. Me and Rocket are in the house next door. You can't find me there, send a prospect for me. I'll always come if you need me, Cecilia."

"Thanks, Lemon. Please tell Apple I'm looking forward to meeting her."

"I will. We'll both come by tomorrow." She

glanced at me with a knowing glance. "Have Bullet here give you some fruit punch. Shit's got a kick to it and it'll help you sleep." She gave a little wave before disappearing out the door.

"Fruit punch?" Cecilia gave me a confused look.

I shrugged. "Got cannabis in it. Kinda makes you, uh, stoned." When her eyes widened, I added hastily. "You don't have to. She's suggesting it because it helped her sleep after she'd been beaten pretty badly a couple of weeks ago. I think she stayed stoned the better part of the next day too. Lemon likes the feel of it and I'm pretty sure she uses it to do unspeakable things with Rocket. But it's not for everyone. Sometimes it helps with pain control. At the very least, you won't care that you're in pain."

She ducked her head. "I wouldn't want to… not be myself if you weren't with me."

I sat on the bed beside her, much as I had in the hospital. "Honey, you don't want me leavin' you, I won't. If you want to try the pot to see if it helps your pain, I'll be at your side the whole time. If you'd rather take conventional pain meds, I can provide that too."

"Either way my wits will probably be muddled."

"Probably, but if you're not comfortable, opioids don't last as long as cannabinoids. Your wits would be muddled, but not for as long."

She winced as she situated herself on the bed. "Maybe I'll try the fruit punch this time."

I grinned. "If it doesn't help or if you don't like the feeling, we'll go to something else."

"Several of the women I know are addicted. Getting beaten up then taking pain pills was how most of them got started."

I understood that all too well. "You trust me to watch over you?" I needed to know. The last thing I'd ever do was leave a person the same as defenseless if they didn't feel safe in their surroundings.

She blinked several times, a shocked look on her face. "Atticus. You've been the kindest person to me since the first day we met. You never talked down to me and you always made me feel like I mattered. Like, if Ettore or Marco killed me, you might miss seeing me. Of all the people in my life, of anyone I've ever known, I trust you the most."

A lump formed in my throat at her words. Knowing that she trusted me above all else hit me hard. It was a responsibility I didn't take lightly. Cecilia wasn't just another patient or person passing through my life. She wasn't even one of my brothers. What she was, was someone I cared deeply about, someone I wanted to protect at all costs. Which meant I was going to annihilate Ettore and this Marco. Whoever he was.

"We need to talk. Do you feel up to it?"

"Sure." She smiled, but she didn't look like she was ready for anything other than food and sleep.

"Hmm. Not sure you're telling the truth there." I frowned as I picked up the napkin from the tray I'd brought. Lemon had placed it over Cecilia's lap, but she hadn't touched it yet. I handed her the napkin before putting the spoon in the soup and scooping up a portion. For some odd reason, I blew on the stuff, so it wasn't too hot for her. Then I held it out for her to eat. Sure, it was something a medical person might do, but I generally left this kind of care up to the nurses, thinking myself too proud. I think I understood now. Cecilia needed help. I provided. No matter what the help was.

She looked surprised, but opened her mouth and accepted the bite. Then I put the spoon back in the bowl and nodded to her, a silent command to eat. She did, thankfully scooping up bite after bite. It seemed like the more she ate the more she wanted. I was glad for her appetite, but I needed to make sure she didn't eat too much.

"Don't go too fast, honey. It's been a week since you've had real solid food. Give your body a chance to acclimate."

"It's really good," she said around a mouthful.

I chuckled. "You certainly make it look good."

"I hope I'm not being too gross."

"Not one Goddamned thing about you is gross, baby."

She took another bite before reaching for a bottle of water. Once opened, she took a good drink. Then she sat back and sighed. "That was really good."

"I'll pass on your compliments to Apple."

"You know, you don't sound like how I imagined a biker would talk."

"Oh?"

"Yeah. 'Course, I guess most bikers ain't doctors."

"Probably not. It's all a matter of the company and the role. Right now, I feel more like your doctor than your protector. Trust me when I tell you, when I go hunting for these fucks, my speech will deteriorate rapidly."

"What?" She sat up straighter, sloshing the soup on her lap. I took the tray and set it aside. "No! You can't go after either of them, Atticus. Please!"

"Why not?" I think I snapped at her more than I intended. I couldn't help it. The thought of being denied that kill nearly drove me to madness.

She gasped, shaking her head again. "Because they'll kill you. They won't stop until they've killed you and everyone and everything you care about."

I leveled a look at her. "You let me worry about that. You worry about healing and getting used to the idea that I've got your back."

Cecilia turned her head to glance out the window. We could see Rocket and Lemon's place several hundred feet away. I knew she had the weight of the world on her shoulders. When she spoke next, there was a defeat that made me want to kill.

"I'm the property of Ettore Alfonso. I'm not important enough to keep alive if one of his associates wants a bit of fun, but I'm valuable enough for him not to let me go as long as I'm alive and useful to him." She sounded dead inside. Not at all like the woman who'd talked with me about *Crime and Punishment*.

I leaned in and gently touched her chin, turning her to look at me once again. "You listen to me, Cecilia. Listen good. I will never keep you prisoner. If you want me to take you someplace away from here, someplace Alfonso doesn't have a foothold, I'll gladly do that. I'll arrange for someone to watch over you if it will make you feel safer. But if you'll trust me, not only will I keep you safe here, I'll make you happy. We're... complicated here at Grim Road. But we're all good men. Honorable men."

"Don't all the women here have to" -- she swallowed --"service the men?"

"No, honey. Are there some here who do? Yeah. But every single woman in that capacity wants to be here. They can transfer clubs if they decide they don't like it here. They can even live here and never have sex with anyone. Naturally, everyone has to pull their weight, but there's a ton of things for everyone to do. Cooking. Cleaning. Helping in the garden. We've got animals that need tending. There's a little girl here who needs a babysitter. Gina does it currently, but I'm sure she would appreciate the help." I held her gaze. "No one will ever force you to do something you don't want to do. Especially not me."

"I liked it," she blurted out. She ducked her head but reached for my hand and held it, stroking the back of my fingers. "What we did before. But I wouldn't want to have sex with anyone else here."

"Rest assured, Cecilia, the last thing you'll ever do is have sex here with anyone other than me, and only with me if you want to. It's pretty much me or be celibate as long as you're here. Just saying." I flashed her a cocky grin. Like I hoped, she let out a small giggle. "Well, that wasn't much, but I'll take it."

"Thank you, Atticus." She stopped and shook her head. "I guess I should call you Bullet."

"Up to you, honey. I think I'm more Bullet than Atticus. Even at the hospital. They just don't know me that way. Well, except for John. Speaking of which, I need to have a conversation with Crush and Byte." I gave her a gentle smile and leaned in to brush a lock of hair off her forehead out of her eyes. "I need to go back to town for an hour or so. I will be back before supper. Do you want me to get Lemon to come stay with you while I'm gone?"

"No. I'll be OK. I'll probably just rest and watch TV or something."

I got up and crossed to the fridge, bringing out a bottle and setting it at her bedside. "If you get to hurting too bad, take a few sips of this. It will take a while to hit, so don't let the pain get away from you. If not, take two pills from the bottle next to it. Just not both." I smiled down at her.

"Maybe I'll wait until you get back?"

"The pills are over-the-counter painkillers. They

won't muddle your brain at all."

"I'll take those, then." She reached for them, taking out two like I'd told her, swallowing them with water. "If I'm still hurting when you get back, maybe I'll try the other drink."

"I swear I won't be long. Just need to make a house call to an old woman. She's not comfortable with her treatment and I promised I'd check on her. Otherwise I wouldn't leave you. Do you understand why I have to go?"

"You make house calls?"

"Only when absolutely necessary. This woman is old and lonely. She wants someone to look after her. I found a nurse to come sit with her a few hours a day, but I'll need to check on her every day for a while. Once she's more comfortable with her new meds, I'll go by to check on her once a week unless she needs something urgently. My goal is to keep her out of the hospital and on her meds. If that means I make house calls, I guess I'll make house calls."

For a long time, she didn't say anything. Just sat there holding my hand and brushing her fingers over mine. She looked so fragile sitting there, much younger than the first time I'd seen her. There was a fighter in there. There had to be for her to have survived the injuries she had. She was hurting, but she'd get her strength back. When she did, we'd come to an understanding. That understanding being she was mine to protect. Even if she didn't want me, I would always protect her.

To the fucking death.

Chapter Eight

Cecilia

The next several days passed in comfortable companionship for me and Atticus. Bullet. I still had trouble thinking of him as Bullet. It seemed to go against his desire to help people. He was always near me. The only time he left me was to check on his patient. I didn't know her name, but he said she was in her nineties. He didn't say much because he was bound by confidentiality not to, but he indicated she was getting better and more confident with her new medication.

I was feeling a lot better. I was still sore, but the bruises were fading and I hurt less and less. I'd also learned a few things about myself.

First, I didn't like how Atticus' fruit punch made me feel. Yeah, I got the giggles and it dulled my pain, but it also made me feel completely out of control. I thought that, had my life experiences not been what they were, I'd have loved the stuff as much as Lemon did.

Second, I was fast falling head over heels for Bullet. Never in my life had a man treated me with so much care and respect. Maybe it was because he was a doctor. Just… something ingrained into his makeup. All I knew was, I'd never felt so cared for and safe. Or respected. We still had conversations about things. Sometimes they were deep and meaningful. Other times fun and silly. And the guy really had a thing for action flicks. I think I gave away a little piece of my heart to him every single day.

Right now, though, he was gone to see his patient, so Apple and I sat in the common room. I wasn't too keen on that room because the women reminded me of so many of Ettore's girls. Some of us tried to stick together, to protect each other, but the truth was Ettore did his best to encourage dissent. It was in his best interest. That way, no one escaped. The club whores seemed to be the same way. All of them thought they'd be queen of the club if they could just score a member high enough.

"I know who you are." One of the girls stopped in front of me, her hands on her hips. She didn't look happy. "You're one of Ettore Alfonso's whores. He finds out you're here, he'll kill us all."

"I think you need to shut up, Chyna." That was from one of the other girls. Apple ignored the whole lot of them, playing on her phone.

"You shut up, Coco. She's a danger to all of us."

"You honestly think Rocket's gonna let some mobster in here? This place is the safest place in the country."

"Don't you know who Ettore Alfonso is? He controls everything on the lower Eastern seaboard. When people go up against him, they die. She's gonna get someone killed just being here."

I sucked in a breath. I hadn't even thought of that. Like it or not, this woman was right. What if Euphemia, the child Lemon had rescued who now lived with the club, got hurt? I'd never forgive myself.

"Get that look off your face, Cecilia." Apple put her phone down and glared at Chyna. "Chyna was just leaving."

"Bitch, you can't make me leave."

"I don't have to. What do you think's gonna happen when my sister hears how you're harassing an old lady in this club? You'll be out on your ear."

"She's not an old lady." Chyna sneered at me, looking me up and down and obviously finding me lacking. "Anyone looking at her can tell what she is. She's a whore. Just like the rest of us. Patched members don't take whores as old ladies."

I shook my head, not wanting to believe what Chyna was saying but knowing it was true. The mafia leaders and enforcers didn't take wives from or claim women who were whores. Double standard? Definitely. But they didn't want every man in the family knowing what their wives were like in bed. Since the men were in charge, the rest of us didn't have a say.

"That's it." Apple stood and advanced on Chyna. The taller woman looked smug, like she didn't believe anyone Apple's size could possibly hurt her. Chyna was at least five ten while Apple wasn't much over five three. But what Apple lacked in brawn, she apparently made up for in spunk.

Before Chyna could react, Apple launched herself at the larger woman. She wrapped her legs around Chyna's middle and used the heel of her hand to pound Chyna's nose.

"What the fuck?" A man stormed into the room and pulled Apple off Chyna. Apple struggled to get out of his arms and back into the fight while Chyna screamed.

"Bitch broke my nose!" she wailed, covering her bleeding nose with her hands.

"Let me go, Spike." Apple kicked back, trying to catch the big man in the knee but missing. Spike didn't look like he was even breaking a sweat.

"When you calm down. You can't go around beating up people. What were you doing?" He sounded like he'd had this conversation a few times. His expression said he didn't usually have it with Apple.

"Teaching a bitch some manners." Apple stilled so Spike let her down. She scrubbed her bloody palm on her jeans before looking down and shrugging. "My suggestion," Apple said as she gave Chyna a death stare, "would be to worry more about minding your own fuckin' business than about some mobster. You want to be part of his fucking stable, go. See how well he treats you compared to this club. But you will stop trying to guilt Cecilia into leaving. She's Bullet's woman and you don't honestly think he got his name because he's a doctor, do you?" Apple kicked the other woman in the shin just as Lemon entered the room.

"The fuck?" She looked from Apple to Chyna and back again. The disbelief on her. Then she scowled. "I'm the badass sister. You're the docile one. Remember? Bad Apple."

Apple grinned at her sister. "You're damned right I'm a bad apple." She nodded to the women who'd gathered around Chyna. "Get the bitches under control, Lemon. Cecilia doesn't deserve their venom."

Lemon looked from her sister to me and back. Then she looked at the gathering of club girls, her expression hardening. "Venom?"

"Same thing they tried to do with me and you. We've got each other's backs. Cecilia is still finding her footing. She doesn't need this shit."

"So you beat the shit outta her?" Lemon looked and sounded confused.

Apple started, then looked back at her sister, an annoyed look on her face. "I'll have you know I'm perfectly capable of dishing out what's needed. I like Cecilia. You said it yourself. We're all gonna be besties. And besties have each other's backs."

Lemon said nothing for a long moment, scowling. Then a grin split her face. "Way to go, sis!

Always knew you had it in you."

I couldn't help but laugh. I covered it with my hand, glancing over at Chyna. "I guess we should get her help. Bullet's gone to see a patient. Is there someone else who could help her?"

"Bullet's the doc," Lemon said with a shrug. "She can put some frozen peas on it or something 'til he gets back. She brought this on herself."

"What do you mean, gone to help a patient?" Chyna asked, her hand still over her bloody nose. "Ain't no one in the infirmary."

"He has a patient from the hospital he's helping with her medicine." I spoke up gamely, genuinely wanting to help Chyna. "I'm not much of a doctor, but I've had to help some of the women I live with after a John got too rough. I'll help you clean up."

Chyna snorted, then groaned as her nose protested. "A patient," she spat. "He's obviously got a woman away from the club he's fucking. No one makes house calls. Are you fuckin' stupid?"

That cut deep. I didn't believe it of Bullet, but we hadn't resumed any kind of personal relationship since he'd brought me here. Sure, I was sleeping in his room, but he usually slept in a chair beside the bed. Or on the couch.

"That's it." Apple took several steps toward Chyna. The other woman cried out in fear and turned and ran out of the room.

Apple followed until, once again, Spike snagged her. "Ease up there, little hellion."

"Someone causing trouble?"

Lemon shook her head. "You could say that, Ringo. Confine Chyna to the club girl's section until further notice. She continues to cause trouble with the old ladies, and I won't have it."

Ringo looked from Lemon to me and raised an eyebrow. "Wasn't aware Bullet had claimed her."

"She's in his room, ain't she?" Lemon's eyes narrowed. "That's enough for me."

"He's not," I said softly. "He's just helping me. Like he is his patient he's gone to see." I blinked, realizing what I'd said. "I mean, assuming that's even where he went." I sniffed, knowing I was about to break down.

Until that moment, I hadn't realized how much I'd grown to depend on Bullet. I remembered our one night and how wonderful he'd been, holding to his word no matter how hard I'd begged. I'd wanted him so desperately that night, needing to experience sex one time in my life with someone of my choosing. He'd been with me, helping me heal inside and out and I was more than attached to him.

I was growing to love him.

Hell. Maybe I was already there.

Chapter Nine

Bullet

"I got what you need, Bullet." Crush popped his head out of his office as I passed. I was heading up to my room to see Cecilia. She wasn't in the common room like normal, but I knew she'd either be with Apple or Lemon. Both women had taken Cecilia into their circle of protection and had done everything they could to make her feel welcome and like she'd found a home. I owed my VP more than I could ever express for that alone.

"You found the bastard?" Crush and Byte had been digging into both Ettore Alfonso and Marco DeLuca. I'd just been waiting for the word for where I needed to go hunting.

"Oh, we've had both of them for a couple days now. Not like their movements are that hard to follow. What we were waiting on was for them to be in a location together."

"Are either of them actively looking for Cecilia?"

"No." Crush shrugged. "Marco thought she was dead. Since she was under Jane Doe during the majority of her hospital stay -- and because of how injured she was, the hospital made her confidential -- they don't know or suspect she survived."

"Good. She'll be safe here while I take care of this."

"I sincerely hope you ain't plannin' on leavin' without tellin' her what you're doin'." Lemon approached from behind us. I knew from the drawl in her voice she was pissed which didn't bode well. For me.

I turned to face her. "I have every intention of telling her where I'm going."

"Good. 'Cause she's hurtin'. And it's your fault."

That caught me off guard. "What do you mean?" I narrowed my gaze, studying Lemon intently. "I've done my best to be as kind and gentle with her as I can. She's healing nicely, but I have no idea the mental trauma she endured."

"Have you talked to her about it? You're the doctor." As she approached, Lemon crossed her arms over her chest. She was a small woman, but her personality was bigger than any of us. She gave orders left and right and continually gave us shit, but Lemon didn't really throw her authority around. She kept us off-balance but that was more for her own amusement. Fun. If you weren't on the receiving end.

"I was trying to give her time to heal. She's got a lot on her plate, Lemon."

"Yep." The woman wasn't backing down an inch. "Surprisingly, most of it has to do with you."

I blinked, not sure I understood where this was going. "What?"

"Get your ass to your room, Bullet."

"Lemon, these guys won't be in one place together long. He's got maybe a couple of hours before the window closes. He could get one and not the other, but given how closely these guys are intertwined, whichever one is left alive will disappear." Crush's gaze moved from me to Lemon and back.

He wasn't wrong. But if Cecilia was hurting because of something I'd done to her, there was no way I could leave her without making it right.

"Where are they?" I turned my attention to Crush as Rocket approached us, a frown on his face.

"At the Playground, if you can believe it. Salvation's Bane could be really helpful."

"A BDSM club." Lemon snorted. "Can they get

more cliché?"

"That's one of Thorn's clubs. Who's his security there?" Rocket put a hand on Lemon's shoulder.

"His name's Lock," Crush said. "Good guy. Steady in a fight. Smart."

"Reach out to Thorn. Let him know who's in their club and see if Lock can find a way to keep them busy without getting anyone hurt." Crush nodded and Rocket turned to me, giving me a look of exasperation. "Well?"

"Well, what?"

"Get your ass upstairs and let your woman know you're claimin' her, dumbass."

I blinked, looking from Rocket to Lemon. "She knows she's mine. She's in my room, ain't she?"

"Did you spell it out to her?" Lemon rolled her eyes. "Like, did you tell her she was your old lady and that you were givin' her a property cut and all that shit?"

"It was implied." I knew the second the words left my mouth it was the exact wrong thing to say. There was no way to stifle the wince. "Never mind. I'm a dumbass."

"Yeah," Lemon agreed. "You are."

Without another word, I took off at a trot to my room on the other side of the compound. I passed several members, all of them looking at me with something between amusement and pity. A couple of club whores approached me, but one look and they backed off.

When I got to the door to my room, I took a deep breath before I announced my presence. The last thing I wanted to do was scare her.

With a shaking hand, I knocked before opening the door. Seconds later, just before I opened the door myself, it was jerked open. Apple stood in the doorway, the spitting image of her sister. Instead of the warm smile and cheery disposition I usually got from Apple, I was met with a fierce scowl Lemon had perfected before she slammed the door in my face. If I hadn't known Lemon was on the other side of the building, I'd have sworn she was with Lemon.

"The fuck?"

I knocked again. There was the faint sound of voices. And a small sob.

"Open the fuckin' door, Apple." I knew in my heart it was Cecilia crying. "Open up the Goddamned door right the fuck now!"

I didn't wait for her to comply. I reached for the knob and tried to open it, but she'd turned the lock. So I banged on the thing again. "Open up!"

"Go fuck yourself!" That was Apple again, but she didn't sound like she was near the door. In fact, I could hear Cecilia's soft sobs. I wasn't sure where she was, but she wasn't next to the door.

I took a breath, then crashed my foot into the door in one hard kick. Apple gasped, but grabbed a glass from a nearby table and hurled it at me.

"You leave her alone!"

I batted the glass away but didn't come any farther into the room. "What the fuck, Apple? I'd never hurt Cecilia and you know it."

"You just kicked in the fuckin' door!"

"Because you locked me out!" I closed my eyes and shook my head. I could not lose my cool. "Apple, do not put anything between me and Cecilia. She's my woman."

Apple eyed me like she was trying to figure out how sincere I was. Then she stepped closer to me. "You hurt her again, I'll fuckin' kill you."

"I didn't mean to hurt her, Apple. She just got away from the bastard who tried to own her. I didn't think she was ready for another man to put a claim on her."

"Dumbass," Apple muttered. "She's not a piece of meat. She's your old lady. At least, she better be. People just think Lemon's the badass. Truth is, Lemon's the one you see coming. Me, on the other hand, I will shank you in your sleep and by the time you realize I'm anywhere around, you'll already be dead." Apple looked back at Cecilia. "You need me, you call me. I will take his fuckin' ass out."

Cecilia nodded but didn't look at either of us. She did take a deep shuddering breath before answering verbally. "I will. Thank you."

When Apple left, I shut the door as best I could with the frame splintered where I'd barged in. It shut, but that was about it. There was no fixing the latch right now.

I took a deep breath before crossing to Cecilia with slow, careful steps. Instead of sitting beside her, I knelt in front of her, reaching for her hand and enveloping it in both of mine.

"Cecilia, honey, please look at me." I tried to be as gentle as I could. The last thing I wanted to do was scare her, or touch her if she didn't want to be touched. When she didn't flinch away or jerk her hand out of mine, I took it as a good sign. After several seconds and brushing away her tears with the back of her hand, she obeyed. "Tell me what I did, so I can make it better."

"I didn't believe Chyna. Not really." Her voice was small and so broken I wanted to pull her into my arms and never let her go. I wanted to shield her from every fucking thing in the Goddamned world.

"What did she tell you?" It was a demand rather than a question.

She shrugged. "Just that no one made house calls anymore. That you were probably going to meet a woman." She sniffed before adding. "One who wasn't a whore. Like me."

"I'm not a good man, Cecilia. Only thing I ain't done for my country is knowingly kill a woman. After this, I'm makin' an exception."

"It's not her fault. I know she was just trying to get under my skin and she did. I mean, she's right that men don't take wives or long-term partners who've been whores. Everyone knows that."

"Honey, men take women they love as their wives or long-term partners. Doesn't matter who they've slept with in the past, or how many lovers they've had. You think I've not fucked more than a few women in my time?"

Again, she shrugged. "Don't seem to matter much. Double standard, but that's the way the world works."

"I guess some men are like that, but I couldn't give two shits. We both have pasts. This is on me because I didn't make things clear to you or anyone else. My only excuse is that I never thought anyone would question you were my woman." I stood and sat on the couch next to her, pulling her onto my lap so I could wrap my arms tightly around her to prove I meant what I said. "I didn't think you'd like having another man claim you as property. It's only phrased that way to show you have my protection. Because I absolutely will protect you. I hope you know that."

"I do. And I know what being property means here. It's not like it was with Ettore. Lemon wears a vest with 'Property of Rocket' on it, but she's also the vice president. Being property doesn't mean a woman is less."

I smiled down at her. "You do get it, don't you?"

"I do. It just hurt to think you might not want me that way. I mean, you never said."

"Puttin' you in my room was enough for everyone to know. Especially the club whores. Well, everyone but the one person who mattered." I leaned in to press my mouth against hers. It wasn't a passionate kiss, just a brushing of my lips against hers. I let the contact linger for several seconds before raising my head to stare into her beautiful face.

The bruises had faded, but there were still a few lingering greenish-yellow splotches. Any cuts or scrapes over her delicate skin had healed, leaving only a slight scabbing that was in the last stages of healing. "Since I didn't make it clear before, I want to now. You're my woman, Cecilia. For as long as you'll have me. I will protect you and treat you like the princess you are. When you're ready, we'll finish what we started the night before you disappeared on me."

"Leaving you that morning was the biggest mistake of my life, Bullet. I wish I could say it was for a selfless reason like protecting you from Ettore if he found you with me, but it wasn't."

"Tell me why you left me, Cecilia." I had to be careful. I wasn't going to call her CeCe even though that was how I'd come to know her. Kicking the door in probably hadn't been the smartest idea I'd ever had, but I had to protect her. Even if it was from herself and all the dark thoughts she had to have running around in her head. I never wanted to hurt her in any way. But I'd do whatever it took to protect her.

"Because I was afraid you'd…" Her voice caught and she cleared her throat before she continued. "That you'd realize how much I didn't deserve you and leave me. I knew after that night I'd never be able to forget you. I wanted to remember it for the wonderful pleasure. Not for you paying me and sending me on my way."

"Christ, Cecilia." I pulled her even closer. I knew I needed to be careful. She might still be sore. But her heartfelt confession was more than I could take. "If anyone don't deserve someone, it's me. You're every single thing I've ever wanted in a woman and more."

She sucked in a breath, two more tears tracking down her lovely face. I brushed the moisture away with the pad of my thumb, wanting with everything in me to simply take her to bed and show her how I felt about her, but I didn't think that was the right move. Not yet.

"Why won't you go further than kissing me now, Bullet?" Her question was so soft I almost didn't hear her. Probably wouldn't have if I hadn't been so close and able to read her lips.

"You want me to make love to you?"

She nodded, then frowned. "I want more than that, actually."

I had to fight a grin. The last thing I wanted to do was give her the impression I was laughing at her or not taking her feelings seriously.

"Honey, all you have to do is tell me what you want and I'll move heaven and earth to make it happen." The corners of my lips lifted in a slight grin. "I'm completely gone on you. All I want is for you to be as happy and content as I can make you."

Another couple of tears spilled from her eyes, but she smiled so I tried not to panic. A woman's tears had never particularly bothered me. I'd witnessed too many times when tears were used as a tool to manipulate. This woman, though... I doubted she was even capable of manipulating me. It should have been a craft she'd perfected over the years as a self-defense mechanism. The fact that she'd left me our first night together instead of staying and trying to get me to protect her told me everything I needed to know about this woman.

"I want you to sleep with me. You know. At night. In the bed with me."

I tilted my head, studying her. "Honey, all you had to do was tell me. I didn't want to freak you out or I'd have been making you sleep in my arms every fuckin' night."

"I want to have sex with you too." She plowed on, and I could actually feel her trembling. Sweat erupted over her skin and I settled her closer, a reflexive action on my part. "Very much."

"All you gotta do is tell me you're ready, honey. Wanted to make love to you that night but didn't want to break my promise." I gave her a cocky grin. "You got one over on me. The last thing I expected you to do was kiss me like that. But, sweet Jesus, that kiss was delicious."

Thank God, that got a genuine smile from Cecilia. And mother fuck, it was glorious.

"God, you're beautiful." My voice came out a mere whisper and with a large helping of awe. "Anything in the fuckin' world I can do to keep that smile on your face I'll do. Don't care what it is, how much it cost, or who I have to fuckin' kill."

"I don't want you to kill anyone." Her smile didn't falter, and I could see how the idea pleased her. The longer she looked at me, though, her eyes widened. "I really mean that, Bullet. I don't want you to kill anyone. Ohmigod! You're actually serious?"

I did laugh then, pulling her even closer to kiss her forehead. "Don't look so shocked, baby. I'm a badass biker."

"You're a doctor!"

"And a biker."

"And a dork." She shifted and I thought she wanted up. When I loosened my hold on her, she shifted to straddle my lap before settling back against me. She laid her head on my shoulder and put her face in my neck. I could feel her lips feathering over my skin.

"You acceptin' my claim, baby girl?"

"I am." The fact that she didn't hesitate told me she was ready.

"You always have the right to say no to anything, Cecilia. I want that straight before we start anything. The only thing I will ever fight you on is something to do with safety. You're mine. That means I keep you safe."

"The fact that you're not willing to compromise on that one thing sets you apart from anything I've been used to. So I accept that stipulation."

"Good. Now. Kiss me and let's seal this deal."

With another glorious smile, she leaned in to give me the kiss I'd demanded of her. If I lived to be a hundred, I promised myself I'd never take her trust -- or her kisses -- for granted. They were a gift. Just like the woman.

As the kiss deepened, I could feel the warmth and passion that built between us. Her hands now firmly grasped the back of my neck, pulling me closer as our lips melded together. This moment had been building up for so long, and it was finally here. I knew that nothing would ever be the same. I drank her sweet kisses, welcoming everything she had to give.

I found myself enveloped in the warmth of her presence, feeling a surge of emotion I couldn't quite place. I hadn't anticipated this level of depth in what had begun simply: two people sharing the love of a tiny outdoor café and stimulating conversation. But as I watched the sun set behind her, I couldn't help but feel an overwhelming sense of joy and contentment. I knew that this was not just a temporary connection, but something much deeper and more meaningful.

She looked up at me with those deep, searching eyes and I knew that she shared the same emotions. Her hand cupped my cheek, her fingers brushing softly over my short beard.

"Don't break my heart, Atticus." She whispered the little plea.

"Never, baby."

She stepped back then, pulling her shirt over her head slowly, only breaking eye contact with me when the material blocked her vision. I rested my hands on her thighs, rubbing gently from the edge of her shorts to her knees and back. The feel of her smooth skin was calming and arousing all at the same time.

When she reached back and unhooked her bra, letting the lacy garment flutter down her arms before she set it aside with her shirt, my breath hitched. Her nipples puckered right before my eyes, and she groaned.

"I've had more men than I care to think about see me naked. Not one of them looked at me like you are right now."

"That's 'cause they had no clue what they had in their arms. If they did, they'd have snapped you up and kept you. Like I'm doin'. I know it's probably too soon, but you need to know I have no intention of ever letting you go. You gonna be good with that?" It was a challenge, pure and simple. To both of us. She needed to know, and I wasn't altogether sure I could pull back even if she protested.

"I know what it means to belong to a man." Her smile slipped, but she looked more intent than haunted. "I have a feeling that belonging to you will be nothing like what I've experienced before. I also think you're a man who takes care of his possessions. You'd never hurt me."

"Damned straight, baby."

Instead of inviting further conversation, she tugged at my shirt, pulling it from my jeans, then over my head. I let her look her fill as she ran her hands over my chest, shoulders, and arms. There was a look of wonder on her face as she traced the tattoos hidden under my clothing. She'd seen my bare chest before, but I suppose in the heat of the moment she hadn't had the chance to explore. I was more than happy to indulge her now.

There was anticipation in her gaze as it drifted over me. Cecilia was practically licking her lips. Then she leaned in and kissed the skin over my pulse and I groaned. I let my head fall back and my eyes slowly drifted shut as she began to explore my skin with her warm tongue, her soft lips following soon after.

The world around me blurred as I closed my eyes, fully immersed in the touch of Cecilia's hands and lips on my skin. My body felt electric, every nerve ending on high alert as I savored the intimacy of her exploration, this closeness with Cecilia while trying to also focus on the moment and the connection we were forming. She smelled so sweet -- almost like strawberries. Her breath was warm against my neck, sending waves of pleasure coursing through my body.

As she moved lower, tracing kisses along my

collarbone and down toward my chest, I gently ran my fingers through her hair, reveling in the silkiness of it against my fingertips.

Her hands roamed up and down my chest and stomach, each touch a spark of electricity that traveled through me and tightened my muscles in response. When she finally reached lower, tugging at the button of my jeans, I helped her pull them down, as well as my boxers, before she sank to her knees to slip between my thighs.

I immediately stiffened, gripping her upper arms. "Cecilia… No. You don't have to do this."

"I know." Her voice was a soft caress as she pulled out my cock and stroked the length, learning the feel and texture. "I need to do this."

"Need?"

"Yeah. Because I want to. You gave me pleasure before. Now it's my turn."

Before I could protest further -- like I really wanted to protest a blowjob from such a beautiful, passionate woman -- Cecilia took the head of my cock into her mouth. I grunted as a shot of precum leaked from the top over her tongue.

"Mmmm…" Cecilia moaned around my dick, her eyes slipping closed as she went to work. She pumped and sucked, slowly at first. She took her time, learning me. Touching me. Looking at the ecstasy on her face, I thought she might be enjoying her gentle exploration. Each time I shuddered as my body gave up another drop of precum, she hummed as if she loved my taste. The experience was almost more than I could take.

"Christ, woman! Fuck!" Sweat beaded over my forehead, as I gripped the edge of the couch like a lifeline. I was about to blow my load, and she'd only been at it a couple of minutes. I wanted to give her anything she wanted -- especially during sex -- but I was not coming down her throat the first time.

I wanted to pull her up to me, but she was sucking on my cock like it was her favorite treat. I gently brushed her hair to the side so I could watch her.

Big mistake.

Her cheeks hollowed as her mouth slid back as she sucked. The only way I could describe the look on her face was one of bliss. It was like she was getting a high or something. I couldn't imagine any woman who'd been forced to do this would love sucking a man's cock the way Cecilia seemed to be.

I shook my head, biting my cheek. I counted back from a hundred. Recited the Declaration of Independence. Anything to keep from ending this with me coming anywhere but in her sweet pussy.

When I could take no more, I reached for Cecilia and gripped her shoulders, pulling her off me. I wanted to fucking sob like a little baby when that warm haven of her mouth left my dick.

"You didn't come..." She looked at me in confusion.

"You bet your sweet ass I didn't come." My voice was more of a growl than anything. Her eyes widened, her lips parting on a cry when I urged her to stand before me. I stripped off her shorts, taking her panties with them.

She stood before me nude, her skin glistening in the light. She was a goddess. I wanted to worship her the entire night. "Never seen the likes of you, woman," I bit out. "So fuckin' beautiful."

"B-Bullet?" She looked unsure, not like the confident woman who'd boldly taken my cock into her mouth and nearly sucked my brains out through my dick. There was no doubt she wasn't used to receiving pleasure. That was something I intended on changing. Starting right the fuck now.

"Ain't takin' you on the couch for the first time, baby." I stood, then lifted her into my arms so she wrapped her legs around my waist. I had one hand on her ass, squeezing just because I could. The other was around her back, holding her to me. "This first time's gonna be pretty Goddamned quick. Ain't never enjoyed a blowjob like the one you just gave me, but I'm on the edge. So I'm gonna make you come, then you're gonna take me with you."

"I -- what?"

Instead of answering, I laid her on the bed before sliding down, trailing my lips over her skin as I wanted. My cock ached like a motherfucker, but I absolutely would not come before she did.

When I reached her pussy, I swiped my tongue through her folds. Her scream echoed through the room, and she bunched the comforter in her fists. I remembered how she'd loved me eating her out before. I wanted her so overcome with pleasure she lost her Goddamn mind. I wanted her to enjoy this so much she wanted to repeat it as often as she could.

As before, she tasted like the sweetest honey. Every lash of my tongue brought more nectar, more gasps and sighs and, finally, screams. I kept her on the edge, never letting her fall over completely until she was covered in sweat and trembling against me.

I crawled up her body, trailing kisses and praising her with every inch. When I finally blanketed her with my large, heavy frame, she wrapped her legs around my waist, holding me tightly to her.

"I need you!"

"I know, baby. I need you too." I reached for the drawer to the nightstand, but she shook her head. "I'm clean. We had to get checked a couple times a month." She looked away, biting her lip uncertainly. "Unless you --"

I silenced her with a kiss, thrusting my tongue deep. "Ain't nothin' more I want than to take you bare. I was only goin' for a condom to protect you. I'm clean, but if you're not on birth control…"

"I am. The shots."

"One last chance, Cecilia. You sure?"

Her legs tightened around me. "I've never been more sure of anything in my life."

I wasn't a saint by any means, and a man can only take so much. With a grunt, I slid inside her in a slow, wet glide to the hilt. She whimpered. I groaned.

"Sweet Jesus," I whispered. "Feel so fuckin' good around me." I kissed her as I moved my hips back and forth. "Hot." Kiss. "Wet." Nip. "Tight…"

"Oh, God!" Her pussy quivered around me and I knew she was there.

"You gonna come, Cecilia?"

"Yes! Bullet!"

"That's it, baby. Squeeze my cum from me."

She did. With a shrill scream, she arched her back, her whole body seizing. I held off as long as I could, until the rhythmic spasms of her cunt made it impossible.

With a harsh groan, I came, unloading my cum into her pussy with sharp snaps of my hips. I shuddered with pleasure so acute it tweaked my gray matter. Something inside me shifted, all of it focused completely on the woman in my arms.

"You're mine, Cecilia. I'll protect you with my Goddamned life. No one in this fuckin' world will ever hurt you again."

I wasn't sure if she heard me or not because she didn't respond at first. Then with a gentle touch to my cheek with her hand, she brought me to her for a soft, sweet kiss.

"Please don't hurt me. I've never mattered to anyone in my life and I was good with that." She took a shuddering breath. "You've made me feel like I matter. If you take it back now, I'm not sure I'd survive."

"You do matter, Cecilia. To me, you... are... *everything*."

Chapter Ten

Bullet

I kissed Cecilia gently as a knock sounded at the door. As I knew it would, the thing opened with the slightest touch. No one entered so I didn't have to kill any of my brothers. Or a fucking club whore.

"Gimmie a sec," I called over my shoulder.

"I'd give you all the time you need, but we're kind of on the clock here."

That was Crush. I knew my club would conduct this mission whether or not I went along, but I wanted to be part of it. I'd seen firsthand exactly how badly they'd hurt Cecilia, and I wasn't going to sit this one out.

"Be there in five."

"You've got three. Then we leave without you." Rocket answered. Which meant, I would not be getting my five minutes.

"Bullet?" Cecilia reached for a pillow to cover herself. I leaned in to kiss her softly before pushing myself off her. I had to hurry, but I would absolutely take care of her.

"Come on, honey. Let's get you cleaned up."

"What's going on?"

I scooped her up and marched to the bathroom, setting her on the vanity before snagging a washcloth. "We're hunting. I have to leave you tonight, but I promise you I'll be back. Hopefully by morning. If not, I'll send someone to let you know what's going on." I cleaned between her legs as I spoke. She still trembled. Likely coming down from the adrenaline rush. I felt like a bastard for leaving her like this. "I'm sorry, Cecilia. I swear, once this is over, I'll spend days worshiping your body like you deserve. This is about taking care of the threat to you."

"Ettore?"

I nodded. "And Marco. They'll only be together for a short time and their location is perfect." I stroked her cheek once before pressing a kiss to her mouth once more. "Come on. I've got to get dressed and get my ass downstairs. I'll send Apple to stay with you. Will you be good with her staying here while I'm gone?"

She nodded, her chin quivering with emotion. "You promise you'll come back?"

"I swear it, honey. I won't be apart from you any longer than I absolutely have to."

"OK." She didn't look or sound OK. "If you promise."

"With all my heart, Cecilia." I kissed her again before hastily pulling on my jeans and a dark shirt. I kissed her one more time, then headed out the door.

Surprisingly, Apple was waiting outside with Lemon. She glared at me before moving past me to the door. Before she could enter my room, I snagged her upper arm.

"Will you please stay with her until I get back?"

"You could stay with her, you know. Rocket and the boys'll bring them back and you can do whatever."

"Because they're not coming back." Surprisingly, it was Lemon who spoke. She looked from Apple to me and back again. I was surprised she seemed to be taking my side in this. It didn't make me feel any better about leaving Cecilia, but this wasn't something I wanted to leave to my brothers.

"She's my woman, Apple. I have to be there to see this through."

Apple rolled her eyes, obviously not happy with either me or her sister. "You better not fuck this up,

Bullet."

"I know what's at stake. Cecilia is mine. She knows it now. She's not happy I'm leaving right now. I get it. She needs reassuring and time to process. But I absolutely will not stay out of this."

Lemon put a hand on my shoulder. "I know what you're going through. I get it." She squeezed my arm. "I'll stay with them." I'd never seen Lemon this subdued. She was almost like a normal person instead of a larger than life one woman wrecking show. "You bring those bastards the justice they deserve."

I cocked my head. "Who are you and what have you done with the vice president of Grim Road?"

Thankfully, Lemon smacked the back of my head. "Nobody likes a fuckin' smartass, Bullet." Better. "Now, get your ass out there before Rocket leaves you."

"Thanks, Lemon. I owe you and Apple after this."

She waved me off. "Not for you. This is for Cecilia."

"I get that. I still owe you."

Lemon held my gaze for several seconds, then nodded her head. "On the house. Get outta here."

A horn sounded outside, and I knew she was right. I needed to get moving.

As I jogged through the clubhouse, several club girls had gathered in the main room. I spotted Chyna among them. She smiled and waved at me even as I glared at her when I passed. I paused at the door and looked over my shoulder. "If you're still here when I get back, I'm gonna forget you're a woman and beat the livin' shit outta you, Chyna. You went too far this time."

Her smile faltered, but I didn't wait any longer.

There were several brothers in the room who could take care of the situation. This was one reason we kept the club girls separate. They were escorted in and out of the grounds if they needed to leave. Also, there weren't many of them. This was a secret compound and we intended to keep it that way.

Outside, I climbed into the SUV Knox had prepped for us. Me, Knox, Rocket, and Scrub were the only members here. Seemed light to me, but I'd never question Rocket on something like this. He knew I had no intention of leaving either target alive and both were big-time mafia. If he thought we were good, we were good.

No one spoke until we got back on the beaten path, on our way to Palm Beach. Then it was Rocket who broke the silence.

"Thorn and Lock at Salvation's Bane have seen to it these fuckers have a private room with four girls they trust. Thorn's only instructions were not to leave any way for these killin's to be tied to the Playground or Salvation's Bane in any way."

"I can handle that." Scrub spoke up, nodding his head. "We doin' it in the room where they're holed up?"

"Yes. Much as I'd love to bring them back and make them last a few weeks, I don't want that kinda heat on us."

"Surprised Thorn's lettin' this go down in one of his businesses."

"Only reason is because Alfonso's been pushin' up on Bane. Tryin' to move them out of Palm Beach. Thorn's tried to meet with the guy to establish some kind of understanding, but Alfonso's workin' with another club. Probably because Thorn refuses to do things Alfonso's way, and he won't pay tribute to

Alfonso. The mob's been harassin' the girls at Salvation's Angels as well as tryin' to run off the high-dollar customers at the Playground." Salvation's Angels was the strip club Salvation's Bane owned, and the Playground was their BDSM club.

"Why's Thorn continuin' to let them in his clubs if they're causin' so much trouble?"

Rocket shrugged. "Bidin' his time. Waitin' for an opportunity to take the fucker out when he wouldn't get his club in the crossfire. We're doin' him a fuckin' favor."

"What's the plan?" I was sure Rocket had already gone over everything with Scrub and Knox before I got there, but I still needed to know.

"I'd make some smartass remark about how you'd know if you weren't upstairs bangin' your woman, but I'm pretty sure she needed to know she's yours." He smirked. "She good?"

"As good as can be. She's healed physically. Still got a few bruises but nothing lasting. The emotional trauma's another story. And I'm not talkin' about only the beatin'. She's got a lifetime of physical, emotional, and sexual abuse to overcome. The main thing is she needs to feel like she's in control of what happens to her body."

"I trust you'll take care of all that?"

"I will. I'll get her any help she needs, and I will always respect her wishes. She may never truly get over everything she's lived through, but I will absolutely be by her side every step of the way."

Rocket nodded. "Good. See you do. Now, as to this little adventure, Ripper and Crush are workin' together to make sure the cameras everywhere over several blocks are take care of. Commercial and private. There will be no evidence we were ever even in the area.

"Once we get to the Playground, Lock and Thorn will take us up through the back of the club to the private room he's letting Alfonso and DeLuca use. We'll take care of them there."

"What about his security?"

"Both men have two bodyguards a piece. Lock says they're pretty attentive, even at the club. Venus is supposed to be takin' care of 'em."

"Venus." I shook my head. "The woman Piston claimed?"

"Yep," Rocket chuckled.

"One woman. Takin' on four mob body men? I know she's a badass, Rocket, but if she can't contain this…"

"This was Thorn's suggestion. Venus is still part of Bane and he trusts her. Worst case, she fucks up and we have to split up to get Alfonso and DeLuca. Might get 'em. Might not. But this means almost as much to Thorn as it does to us. It's in his best interest to take these guys out."

I shrugged. "Guess that'll have to be good enough."

"Good."

The rest of the ride was done in silence. We each had a piece, but if things went right we wouldn't use them. Last thing we wanted to do was discharge a firearm in a crowded club. Not only would the chance of collateral damage be unacceptable, but we didn't want to draw attention to ourselves.

We left Knox in the SUV three blocks away from the club. Several city lights were out in two separate directions from our location going to the club. No doubt Ripper and Crush's doing. It gave us an alternate route to and from the club so we could stay in the shadows.

As we approached the back, we met Venus as she strolled out of the building like she didn't have a care in the world. She was dressed in her ever-present pink. This time with pink dreadlocks instead of the long curls she normally sported. The woman was tall and solidly built, but compact. Muscular without being overly so. She had the body to back up any skills she had. Definitely not a woman to fuck with.

"Way is clear. You have at least half hour before bodyguards miss check-in." She nodded at Rocket but didn't break her stride. "See you back at club."

"Ain't going back to Bane, Venus," Rocket said.

"Me neither."

I missed a step. Rocket looked over his shoulder and narrowed his eyes.

"I got a bad feelin' about that," I muttered.

"Yeah." Rocket shook his head but kept moving. I thought I saw him fighting a grin, but it could have been a scowl.

Once inside, the driving bass of the music pounded through me, even away from the main room where the speakers belted out a rhythm. I was wrong. We could probably have a whole entire fire fight upstairs, and no one would notice.

Lock met us and jerked his head for us to follow him. He took us up to the third floor. The music wasn't as obnoxious but still ever present. He took us to the end of the hall where Thorn stood outside the door. Two men lay at his feet while Blood, the sergeant at arms of Bane, and a couple other men were busy packing them into bags to be moved out.

Scrub moved around us to Blood's side and the two men conversed while Thorn and Rocket greeted each other.

"They're so high I doubt they'll give you much trouble." Thorn shook his head. "I really expected gettin' rid of these guys would be harder than this. I've got everyone in my club in the immediate vicinity staked out around both here and in the blocks surrounding the club, as well as Alfonso's headquarters. All his underbosses and capos are where they're supposed to be with the appropriate number of men with them." He shrugged. "They must have a really poor opinion of us."

"What about the MC they're partnered with? They accounted for?"

"Yeah. Fortunately, the club's still pretty small. We took out most of the players several years ago, but the cockroaches keep comin' back. This time, I'm pretty sure Alfonso's put one of his men in charge. I've got eyes on 'em. They had a couple members in here tonight, but Venus took care of 'em." Thorn hesitated a moment before he continued. "Expect a visit from her."

"Visit?" Rocket stiffened. "Christ, I feel a nightmare comin' on."

"Hey, man." Thorn grinned. "What'd you expect when you made your old lady your vice president? The women smell blood in the water and are headed your way."

I'm not sure what I expected Rocket to say or do, but the laugh he barked out wasn't it. "If she's even half of what you say she is, you're lucky she's not runnin' your show."

"Yeah, well, it was touch and go for a while, but I convinced her we were small potatoes. Told her if she wanted a real badass club, she needed to head to you guys or Iron Tzars." The other man had a grin from ear to ear.

"You givin' your blessin' if she wants to patch

in?"

"In all seriousness, I hate to lose her. Venus is one of the best assets we've got. But if she wants to patch into another club, I'd never stand in her way."

"Figured she'd end up with her sister in Bones."

"Well, it wasn't for lack of trying. Millie threatens to take her back to Kentucky every time she visits."

Rocket nodded to the door. "You ready?"

"Knock yourself out, brother."

Rocket entered the room first. The women entertaining the two mafia men were pushing a steady supply of cocaine on them. Both men were partaking, laughing, and looked like they were having the time of their lives. They didn't even notice we'd slipped in.

The girls noticed. Instead of acknowledging our presence, they kept the men focused on them, keeping Alfonso and DeLuca between us and them.

Rocket took out a phone Crush had given me and snapped a few pictures to send to Byte for positive ID on the men. The last thing we wanted was to kill the wrong men. Not that I'd personally mind. If they were part of Alfonso's bunch -- even if they were decoys -- I could give a good Goddamn. But I wanted Alfonso dead for what he'd let DeLuca do to Cecilia.

It took less than a minute for Rocket to hear back from Byte and Crush. He nodded at me, and we each took one man. The girls didn't make a sound. We didn't kill them. We weren't ready for that yet. I wanted both men to know why they were getting ready to die.

Securing them wasn't hard. They both fought, but the drugs and the fact that both Rocket and I were much stronger and more skilled than either of these men made all the difference. Once we had them under control, I moved around in front of them. Rocket ushered the girls out and waited just inside the room until I finished this.

While this floor wasn't as noisy as the floors below, Thorn had assured us no one was on this floor tonight, courtesy of the two men I was about to murder. I removed their gags and stood back to face both men.

"You're getting ready to die," I said without preamble. "I just want you to know why."

"My men will fuckin' kill you, you son of a bitch!" Alfonso bit out the threat while DeLuca gave me a death stare.

"Your men won't have a clue what happened to you. As we speak, there are people setting it up to look like you left this club and went to the docks. No one will know you met your end here."

"Do you have any idea who I am?" Marco DeLuca looked faintly amused as he questioned me, but Alfonso was just angry. I had no doubt he expected to walk out of here alive. Sucked to be him.

"Yeah. I do." I grinned. I'm sure it wasn't a pleasant look. "I just don't give a fuck." I shifted my gaze to Marco DeLuca. "You're going to die first, since you're the one who beat Cecilia and left her for dead. Then your friend, Ettore Alfonso over there" -- I jerked my head in Alfonso's direction --"is gonna die for giving you the go ahead to do what you wanted with her."

"Cecilia." DeLuca said her name like he had no idea who I was talking about. Then he snorted. I could see the comprehension on his face. "CeCe? This is about a whore?"

"This is about a young woman you hurt."

"A whore." He actually chuckled and I had to

restrain myself from snapping his neck right then. That would let him off too easily. "That must be one prime piece of pussy."

"The more you talk, the harder you die," I said.

He shrugged. "How much?"

"Excuse me?"

"How much do you need to compensate you for the whore?"

"I'm sorry, did you think you could buy your way out of this?" I grinned as I took a step closer. "The only reason you're not already dead is because I wanted you to know why you were about to die. Trust me. This is happening."

I moved around behind DeLuca while he sputtered. "You're a fuckin' dead man, motherfucker. A fuckin' dead man!"

"Not as dead as you." With deliberate slowness, I positioned my hands. One on top of his head, slightly above his left ear, the other on his chin. I held the position for several seconds before jerking his chin up and to the left and shoving his head to the right, effectively snapping his neck.

I moved back around in front of him. DeLuca's eyes were wide. He looked from side to side but was unable to breathe or move.

"Ah, look at that." I said conversationally to Alfonso who'd started swearing the second he heard his partner's neck break. "He's still conscious. Could be a couple minutes before he dies." I grinned. "Perfect."

"You fuckin' cocksucker! Motherfucker!"

"I believe it was you who insisted this floor be closed off tonight." I was enjoying this way too much. "With all the noise downstairs -- and the fact this is a BDSM club -- scream all you want. Anyone who hears you will assume you're playing. But it's doubtful anyone will hear."

"You can't do this! My men will fuckin' kill you!"

"Well, they'd have to know who I was first. Then they'd have to be able to find me. That, however, doesn't matter because it will be days -- weeks even -- before your men even know you're dead."

DeLuca's eyes had stopped moving and his face was turning blue. I wasn't sure if he was dead yet, but it was inevitable. I moved behind Alfonso, positioning my hands in the same position.

"Any last words?"

"Give me a number! Name your price, you bastard!"

"Odd last words, but to each his own." I snapped his neck the same way I had DeLuca's, then moved around to face both men. Unlike his partner, Alfonso was dead instantly. I checked the pulses of each man. Neither had one.

"Is it done?" Rocket's voice was matter-of-fact, no emotion at all. Rocket was no stranger to killing. It hadn't been that long ago they'd taken apart one of our own men. Literally. There were so many pieces of him, disposal would have been as simple as tossing him into the ocean. Scrub had done a more thorough job, of course. But two men with two broken necks was nothing to him. Or me.

"Yep. they're dead. No surprises."

"Good. Let's go."

We exited the room to find the other bodies gone and Scrub and Blood waiting outside. "I'll be along in a bit," Scrub said. "Me and Blood will take care of the bodies."

"I'll send Knox back for you. Pretty sure Bullet wants to get back to his woman."

"Works for me. This will take us a couple hours."

Thorn stuck out his hand to Rocket who took it in a firm grip. "Thanks for the help."

"Was gonna say the same to you."

"Mutual satisfaction, then."

"Agreed."

Chapter Eleven

Cecilia

The wait for Bullet to come back was the longest of my life. In reality, I'm sure it was only a couple hours. Felt like days. Not only was I worried sick about him, but what if he didn't come back?

I trusted him with my life. My fear stemmed from my insecurities. My fears of abandonment and feeling of unworthiness. I was surprised I hadn't had any hang-ups about sex with Bullet, but I didn't. I'd wanted sex with him like I wanted my next breath. Probably because, for the first time in my life, I realized how pleasurable sex could be.

I paced around the room I shared with Bullet. Lemon and Apple tried to distract me, but I couldn't concentrate. Also, I was sure I'd bitten my nails down to the quick.

The door opened and Bullet entered. My breath caught. I wanted to run to him, but I couldn't seem to move. My breath came out in little pants and I got dizzy. Immediately, Bullet moved to me, picking me up in a big bear hug as he moved across the room to a chair and sat with me on his lap.

"Everything go OK?" I thought that was Lemon talking to Bullet, but I wasn't sure. Bullet was back. He was safe. If Ettore and Marco were dead, so much the better. But the only thing that mattered to me was that Bullet was home and in one piece.

"Yep. All went according to plan. Rocket was right behind me. He can fill in all the details you want."

I felt a hand on my shoulder, which was when I realized I was crying on Bullet's shoulder.

"Cecilia? You good? I'll stay if you want." I

looked up to find Apple standing over us. She had a concerned look on her face, but I could tell she knew I was OK. She just wanted verbal conformation.

"Yeah. I'm all good now." I gave her a watery smile. "Thank you both for staying with me. I'm not sure my sanity would have survived otherwise."

"We'll always have your back, Cecilia." Apple smiled and leaned in to kiss the top of my head. Then she spoke to Bullet. "You take care of her."

"It'll be my privilege and pleasure to take care of her, Apple. Thank you. You and Lemon are perfect for this club."

Lemon snorted. "Of course, we are. We're fuckin' awesome."

That got a laugh out of me. Which seemed to be what the sisters were waiting for because they both left.

"Are you really OK? You didn't get hurt?"

"No one laid a finger on me, honey."

I hugged him tight. "I was so worried!"

"I'm sorry I had to leave you, Cecilia. We had them both in a place we could control and had to take it while we could."

"I'm just thankful you're home safe."

"You're safe now, Cecilia. I'll give you this one chance to..." He cleared his throat and shook his head. "Fuck."

"What?" I pulled back, needing to look at him. What was he thinking? "What is it?"

"I was gonna say I'd give you this one chance to leave so you could have a normal life, but I can't."

"Can't what?"

"Let you go. Last thing I want to do is keep you against your will, but I swear to you, Cecilia. I'll do whatever it takes to make you happy and wanting to stay with me."

I just looked at him, not sure what to think or say. "Why would you think I didn't want to stay with you?"

"I'm not going back to the hospital. In fact, I doubt I'll even have a private practice anymore. We'd be here most of the time. As a rule, I'm the only one who travels much into the city and I usually stay at my house, only coming here when the guys need me." He shook his head. "Not anymore. Grim Road is a safe place. The rest of the world ain't. I want you protected."

"As long as I'm with you, I know I'm safe, but that's not why I want to stay with you, Bullet." I took a breath. "You're the first person to make me feel like I actually matter. I'm selfish enough to not want to give that up. So, I'm holding you to your promise not to let me go."

"Just try to get away from me." Bullet smiled and something inside me... eased. It was like a band that had been tightening around my chest over time. I hadn't realized it was smothering me until the pressure was gone. I took in a big gulp of air and let it out. Then I wrapped my arms around him and sobbed against his neck.

Bullet rubbed my back, murmuring softly while the dam broke. He didn't try to hush me or stop sobbing my heart out. Once the storm had passed, he handed me some tissues. His smile was kind and so full of an emotion I was afraid to name, I wanted to cry all over again. Never had a man looked at me like Bullet did.

He leaned in, pressing his lips to mine tenderly. His tongue darted out to lick my lower lip and I opened for him. Bullet kissed me until my head was spinning before he pulled back and pressed his forehead to mine.

"I love you, Cecilia. I swear I'll make you happy."

"You already do, Atticus. I didn't want to admit it to myself, but I fell in love with you the first time we talked at that café. You never treated me like a whore even though you had to know what I was."

"Like I told you before, honey. You're a beautiful, intelligent, wonderful woman. And now you're all mine."

I smiled. "I love the sound of that."

Bullet took me to bed then. As he promised before he'd left, he spent the next two days worshiping my body. We came out for meals and for him to parade me around the common room where the club girls could see us together. Chyna was noticeably absent, and the other women kept their distance from both Bullet and Rocket. I wanted to ask, but honestly, I could give two shits as long as they stayed away from him.

* * *

"Things are startin' to shake up, prez." Crush had been in his office since we came back from killing the mafia men who controlled the lower Eastern seaboard. He'd been monitoring shit and keeping an eye on this section of the Italian mafia in case there was blowback.

Rocket was sprawled in a chair with Lemon sitting in his lap giving the guys hell while we watched, laughing at how disgruntled a few of them looked. It was a game they played and was amusing to no end. "Yeah? What's up?"

"A whole lot of confusion. The underbosses tracked them to Port Palm Beach, but couldn't find the bodies, or any trace of them from there. Looks like Blood from Bane and Scrub did their jobs right."

"You really expected anything different?" Lemon looked amused.

"Nah." Crush waved her off. "Just passin' on the information. There's a power void, though. Someone's gonna have to step in to fill it."

"Two guesses who that's gonna be," Lemon snorted.

"My bet's on Thorn." Mace, one of the men I'd recently met spoke up, tilting his beer bottle in Lemon's direction. "His city. His pain in the ass."

"Nah." Bear waved Mace off. "Thorn might operate on the wrong side of the law sometimes, but he ain't interested in that shit. If you ask me, it'll be Sting from Iron Tzars."

Lemon barked out a laugh. "I thought you were the smart one, Bear. I mean, you nominated me for VP. You had to be smart. But that's the dumbest thing I've ever heard you say. Sting don't give a shit about that kind of stuff. Besides, he might have a hidden chapter close by, but he's in Indiana. He can't take over the place from Indiana."

"Why not? Alfonso had his share of human trafficking. Sting's all about taking that shit down. If they've got a chapter close by, might be in their best interest to at least look into stepping in."

"Which he would. But he's not interested in running the rest of Alfonso's operation. No. If you ask me, it'll be El Diablo. He's already got mafia ties, of sorts, and the brains, connections, and resources to get a stranglehold on the entire region."

"She's got a point." Byte had followed Crush in and leaned against the door frame. "Explains some of the moves we've seen. Wrath, who's also the district attorney for the area, has been quietly moving assets and filing contracts for all kinds of shit. I don't understand the legal shit, but it looks like there are several shipping companies with new majority shareholders that do business exclusively with companies shipping into and out of Port Palm Beach."

"Huh." Rocket snorted. "I bet if you look further into that, you'll find where someone got Alfonso and DeLuca memberships to the Playground or something. My guess is, the other night was set up to make it easy for us to kill those two."

"Makes sense. How else would two of the most powerful men in the mafia be that easily picked off?"

"Score one for the Devil, I guess." Rocket leaned in and kissed Lemon's cheek.

"Got a question for you, Crush." Bullet frowned as he spoke. "How does John Mason know you and Byte?"

Crush looked uncomfortable but merely shrugged. "He's... I guess you could call him our mentor? Raised us. Encouraged us to go into the military. I think he's got some kind of tie with Mama and Pops at Bones, though my understanding is they don't talk to each other."

"You know why?"

Crush shrugged. "Nope. Not my business."

Rocket shifted Lemon around so she straddled him, then stood with her in his arms. "Don't know. Don't give a fuck. Time to go fuck my woman."

That got laughs from everyone.

"Sounds like a good idea. Think me and Cecilia'll do the same."

I laughed, snuggling closer to Bullet as he stood and carried me from the room. With a sigh, I latched onto his neck with my mouth, sucking softly.

"Woman, I'm gonna fuck you all night."

"Good. 'Cause I'm gonna fuck you all night too."

"Damn straight you are. Might fuck you all day tomorrow."

"Promises, promises…"

Somehow, he got the door open to our room, then took me inside, kicking the door shut behind him. We made short work of our clothes. I soon found myself on my hands and knees with Bullet mounting me from behind.

The sex was fast and furious, but no less pleasurable than it was when he took his time. No matter what we did, no matter how many times he fucked me, Bullet always made sure to give me as much pleasure as he could. And sex with him was always pleasurable.

When we were both spent, Bullet rolled us to our sides, his cock still firmly inside me as he pulled me close, spooning me against him. He sometimes did that. Held me until I fell asleep with his cock still inside me, only to wake me a little while later with slow, steady thrusts until I came again.

We were both breathing hard as he pulled the comforter around us, tucking it in around me before settling himself. I think I drifted off before I felt him slip something onto my finger.

"Bullet?"

"Shh, baby. Go back to sleep."

Of course, I didn't. I raised my hand to look at the ring he'd placed on my finger. It was a simple diamond solitaire on a gold band. The gem was the perfect size for my finger. Not too big. Not too tiny.

"What's this?"

"You know what it is." His voice was gruff with emotion. Or maybe it was where he'd just come his brains out and bellowed to the rafters.

"I know what it looks like, but you never said."

"It's an engagement ring."

I waited for more... like, you know, "Will you marry me?" but it never came.

"Uh, aren't you forgetting something?"

"Nope."

"Bullet! You're supposed to ask me to marry you."

"Am not."

"Are to! What the fuck?" I tried to move, but he just grunted and tightened his hold on me.

"Stay still. Sleep."

"Bullet --"

He cut me off. "Askin' means you could say no. Ain't askin'."

I blinked, trying to process what he'd just said. Then I laughed. God, I loved this man!

"Ain't nothin' funny about it. You're marryin' me."

"Never said I wasn't."

"Good. Now that we've settled that, my young, soon-to-be-wife has worn me out. I'd like a nap before I fuck her again."

I giggled and sighed happily. "Fine. But next time, I get to be on top."

"I'm down with that."

I loved my life...

Knox (Grim Road MC 4)
A Bones MC Romance
Marteeka Karland

Evelyn: My life fell apart right before my eyes. The fire and losing everything we had was bad enough, but when my boyfriend's father convinces me to go to the hospital, the one thing me and my kids had left evaporates like a plume of smoke when I see their father with his... pregnant wife. Not only do I feel like a complete fool, I'm left to explain things to my children. Then there's Knox. He's my boyfriend Danny's older brother. The one everyone thought was dead. The one who is an older, bigger, scarier version of Danny. He is so gentle with me and my children, so protective when he has no reason to be. He's also the man I have no hopes of resisting.

Knox: I let my family think I was dead for fifteen years. There were multiple reasons. Not the least of which was securing a steady income for my father after Danny blew through everything he had. I tried to keep tabs on them, especially after Mom died, but I didn't dig deep enough. As a result, Danny's girlfriend, Evelyn, is in the crosshairs of something very sinister. Once I find out who's responsible, there will be hell to pay. No matter who brought death to those I love, I will make them pay. When I do, I'll be putting the loyalty of my club to the test. When it's all over, I hope Evelyn will be able to forgive me. Because I've fallen in love with my brother's woman and no one will come between us. No one.

Chapter One

Evelyn

Fire.

Smoke.

I clung to Luke and Aneshya, trying my best to shield them from the chaos around us. We coughed as we tried to make our way down the hall, but the smoke was so thick, it was pitch-black inside the cramped space.

"We've gotta get out of here!" Mr. Knoxville from across the hall was the children's grandfather. The man always looked out for us, even when his son couldn't. "Evelyn!"

"We're over here!" I clutched my children close. We had a damp bed sheet over the three of us, but it wouldn't do much for long. The smoke was getting thicker and there was no way a bed sheet was going to protect us from fire. "I can't find Danny! He was just here!" I coughed and coughed as I sucked in a lungful of smoke with every breath. Luke tried to push me down, but I resisted. I needed to get my family to safety and that included Danny.

"Mommy, we need to go!" Aneshya sounded frantic, a round of coughing taking her as well. Luke stopped shoving at me and blanketed his sister, taking her to the floor.

"Crawl, Aneshya! Mom! Come on! Now!" Luke was only twelve, but he was protective of both me and his sister. "Grandpa! Make Mom follow us!" He tried to take charge and I knew he was right. But my long-term boyfriend and the kids' father, Danny, had been beside me only a moment before. I couldn't just leave him.

Mr. Knoxville suddenly appeared in front of me.

He was in his late seventies, but the man was fit and strong as an ox. And protective as they came. I thought it might be where Luke learned it from. If Danny had inherited the trait from his father, he never showed it to me. Or the kids, really. As evidenced by the fact that it was his father and son trying to take care of me and Aneshya instead of Danny.

"Don't worry about him, Evelyn." Mr. Knoxville looked hard and almost dangerous. When he looked like this, it made me want to do anything he said without question. "He's a grown man. You've got to get the children out. Now!"

"But Danny --"

"Will be fine. Or he won't. Your first priority -- *my* first priority -- is you and the children." I'd never heard Mr. Knoxville speak so harshly to me. He was always the one to help me when Danny didn't come home. Or when Danny got mean. The kids were older, but I didn't like leaving them alone. Mr. Knoxville was always so sweet and kind. But then, this situation didn't call for sweet and kind. "Now get them and yourself out of here, Evelyn! Now!"

Luke and Aneshya were crawling on the floor down the hallway of our apartment building. Mr. Knoxville pushed me to my belly and urged me to crawl after the kids. The smoke was more tolerable low to the ground but still surrounding us. I choked with every breath. The fire was mostly behind us, but it was spreading. I thought I could hear sirens off in the distance.

"Keep movin', girl! Don't stop!"

"Luke!" I called out to my son, the smoke so thick and dark I'd lost sight of him and Aneshya as I lagged behind.

"We're at the stairs!" Luke coughed again, his

voice faint in the distance separating us. I could hear Aneshya coughing too. I hated that they had trouble breathing but was also grateful they were on the move. "Hurry, Mom!"

"I'm coming, Luke!" I crawled faster. Mr. Knoxville touched my ankle, urging me forward each time I hesitated. "Keep going! Get your sister out!"

"You keep goin' too, girl. We're gonna get outta here!" Mr. Knoxville's voice was tight, and he coughed several times as he continually shoved me along.

The roar of the flames was growing louder. Heat billowed in a great rush from the flames I was certain were ready to bear down on us.

I heard the children cry out. Pain? Were they hurt?

"LUKE! ANESHYA!" When I sucked in another breath to scream again, I breathed in smoke which started a coughing fit. My lungs burned and spasmed, making it nearly impossible to take in another breath. I tried to keep moving, but it was all I could do to breathe. Panic tightened around my neck. With the smoke suffocating me, it really felt as if someone were actually strangling me.

I stumbled to my feet, needing to get to my kids as fast as I could and crawling wasn't getting it done. I called out to them with every breath I could suck in. Then strong hands grabbed my shoulders. In the blackness of the smoke all around me, those hands were the first indication I had there was someone in front of me.

"Get down." The gruff voice was muffled, and I realized he had on a mask. Firefighter? Then he shoved me back to the floor and pushed me to give me direction. "Keep crawling that way. The stairs are a few yards in front of you."

"My children! Did you see --"

"They're on the way out."

"Mr. Knoxville's behind me --"

"I'll get him."

"Danny --"

"I said go, woman! We'll be right behind you." He urged me onward, and all I could do was crawl in the direction he said. I hoped, since he'd sent me in that direction, he knew the way was clear. I trusted that my children were in that direction.

The farther I went, the heavier the smoke. Right up until I descended half the flight of stairs on my hands and knees. Coughing, I stood and hurried as fast as I could. With the receding smoke, it was easier to breathe. To move.

"Mom!"

"Luke?" I sobbed in relief as I recognized my son's voice.

"There she is, Luke!" Aneshya sounded strong. Not like she'd been hurt or couldn't breathe.

Then I was in the arms of my son, my daughter clinging tightly to me as they moved me out of the apartment building. I barely made it out into the grass before I collapsed, my legs finally giving out. I clutched Aneshya to me as tightly as I could. Luke had his arms around me but was still trying to get me to move farther away from the building.

"It's not safe here, Mom. We need to get farther back."

"Mr. Knoxville." Panic filled me. Did the older man get out? "He was right behind me. Where is he?"

"The fireman said he'd make sure you both got out." Aneshya tugged at me, following her brother's lead as usual. "Come on, Mom. Let's go."

Each breath seemed to bring on more coughing,

but I sucked in a deep breath of clean air and managed to get the coughing mostly under control. "Where are the other firemen?" I looked around, not seeing anyone other than a few bystanders. I could hear sirens off in the distance getting closer, but no one was here yet.

"Not sure," Luke said with a frown. "But he said he would get you and Mr. Knoxville out and for us to go on."

"We were waiting for you." Aneshya's voice broke and tears made tracks through the streaks of soot on her face. "I thought you'd gotten lost."

It was then Mr. Knoxville stumbled through the same exit we'd managed to escape through. The fireman was right behind him.

"Mr. Knoxville! Oh, my God! Are you all right?" I hurried in his direction, trying to put the man's arm around my shoulders so he could lean on me if necessary. I should have known better. My knees were weak already. There was no way I could hold the older man's weight. Instead, I found him holding me up with an arm around my waist as he urged us farther away from the building which was engulfed in flames.

The guy coming up behind Mr. Knoxville was huge. He towered over all of us and was solidly built. He still had on a full-face mask with SCBA gear but I could see his face through the clear plate. The man looked familiar, but I couldn't quite place him.

"Please! My boyfriend, Danny! He's still in there somewhere!"

Instead of going back inside immediately, he turned to Mr. Knoxville.

"Up to you." Mr. Knoxville had leaned over with his hands braced on his knees while he coughed, same as the rest of us. "Fuckin' prick left his children in a burnin' fuckin' buildin'."

"What?" I gasped in surprise, looking up at Mr. Knoxville. Not only had I never heard the other man swear like that, but he was accusing Danny -- his own son -- of deserting us in a crisis. "No! Danny and I have had our problems, but he'd never leave his kids. We got separated. He's still in there. Probably looking for us! You have to find him!"

The firefighter took off the mask, and it was like I was looking at a slightly older, bigger, much scarier version of Danny. I sucked in a breath...

... then immediately started coughing. Luke was at my side when I collapsed on the ground on my knees. I fell forward onto my hands in the grass, coughing uncontrollably.

"We need to get Mom to the hospital." Luke handed me a bottle of water. I had no idea where that came from, but I took a gulp before promptly coughing again. I glanced over at Aneshya. She had a worried expression on her face but wasn't coughing anymore. Luke looked like he wasn't hurt either, but I had to be sure. Both of them were streaked with soot.

"Are... you..." I gasped. "Are you... hurt?"

"No, Mom." Luke was quick to reassure me. "Aneshya's fine too. Drink some more."

The next thing I knew an oxygen mask was placed over my face and the Danny look-alike was in front of me, holding my gaze with a steady one of his own.

"Take deep breaths, honey." He put what looked like an inhaler in the hole at the side of the mask and squeezed it. I felt the mist from the spray enter my lungs as I inhaled. I still coughed, but after a few seconds, the pressure in my chest relaxed a little. After another lungful of air and more coughing, he did it again. After that, it wasn't long until the pressure in my chest eased almost entirely. I still coughed, but it felt different. Like the coughing was actually helping to clear my lungs instead of being a futile effort.

"Mom?" Aneshya looked up at me with worry in her expression. She'd wiped her face with something, washing some of the soot off, but smearing it over her face.

"I'm okay, sweetie."

"Fire and EMS are on the way." The man kneeling in front of me moved the mask long enough to urge me to drink some more water before replacing the mask. "Just take some slow, deep breaths. I gave you an inhaler. Got something to help with the spasms in your lungs. Might make your heart race a bit, but nothing too bad."

"Who are you?"

He glanced over at Mr. Knoxville who was looking at him with a combination of pride and relief. If there were tears in the gruff old man's eyes, I was sure it was from the smoke. "Denver. Boy..."

"It's Knox." He stood before his face split into a grin. "It's good to see you, Pop."

"Fuckin' Christ, Denver!" Mr. Knoxville pulled Knox close, and the two men clapped each other on the back heavily, sharing a chuckle and a warm embrace.

"Denver?" Luke asked, his eyes narrowing. "Dad's older brother?" He shook his head slowly. "You're dead." Then he shifted his gaze back to his grandfather. "Or did you and Danny lie to us!" It was a demand instead of a question.

"He didn't lie," Knox said as he and Mr. Knoxville separated, still gripping each other's shoulders as if reluctant to let go. "It's complicated." Then he knelt beside me again. "Better?"

I couldn't speak. I was just trying to breathe. But

yeah. I felt better so I nodded several times.

"Good." Again, he removed the mask long enough to give me some more sips of water. "Luke, I'm in the older black Ford truck with an enclosed black trailer behind it. In the trailer you'll find a stack of clean cloths in a clear tote. Bring a handful along with some more bottled water. It should all be just inside the door of the trailer."

Luke looked at his grandfather before looking back at me. "I don't know. I think I should stay with Mom while you go get whatever you want."

"It's all right, Luke." Mr. Knoxville gave Luke a serious look. He wasn't dismissing the older boy's worries. More like reassuring him. "I'll stay with Evelyn."

"I don't know..." He looked from his grandfather back to Knox again.

To his credit, Knox didn't try to hurry Luke or in any way dissuade him. Instead, he waited patiently for Luke to make up his mind.

"Mom? Will you be all right?"

I tried my best to smile. My chest still hurt, but it was more like my insides were raw and scraped. No doubt from smoke inhalation. I nodded, pulling the mask away once more. "I'll be fine, honey. Why don't you take Aneshya with you? She can help you."

That seemed to be what Luke needed, though he still looked worried. Likely he saw this as an opportunity to get his sister away from a strange man where he could find a safe place for her to wait until he could come back for me.

When the children were gone, Knox turned his full attention on me. It wasn't a very comfortable place to be. He looked so much like Danny, but where Danny was slender and leanly built, Knox was large and thickly muscled. He had a few scars on his face. Nothing too horrible, but enough to give him an edge and make him look rugged and battle-hardened. The thing was, he could be Danny's twin. If I remembered correctly, Denver -- Knox -- was older than Danny -- seven or eight years older. The most uncomfortable thing of all, though, was the fact that this man looked at me with a concern I'd never seen from Danny. While we got along well -- not even verbal arguments -- Danny wasn't an overly demonstrative person. In fact, he wasn't at home much because he worked constantly. I had my own job, but I mostly worked from home. Whatever we had never seemed to be enough for Danny. He always wanted more and worked hard to have whatever those things were.

Instantly, my gaze went to Mr. Knoxville. He knew Danny was never home. It was why he made sure we all lived so close to him. So we had someone close if we needed them. Mr. Knoxville was big on taking care of his family, and I'd been more than grateful for the help he'd given me when I'd had to be gone for short periods and he'd kept an eye on things.

"He's not like Danny, Evie. I swear it. Denver… er… Knox… takes care of his own. That includes you and his niece and nephew, too, now that he's back." The older man gave his son a look that said there would be a come-to-Jesus meeting. Soon.

Knox narrowed his gaze on Mr. Knoxville. "What're you gettin' at, old man?"

Mr. Knoxville just shrugged. "A discussion for another time. We need to get Evelyn to the hospital."

Knox nodded slowly, but I didn't think he was agreeing with his father. More like he acknowledged the fact that now wasn't the time. But I got the feeling he still intended to keep his secrets. No matter what his father wanted.

Luke and Aneshya hadn't returned. I knew Luke had no intention of bringing his sister back until he was certain Knox wasn't a threat to us. Knox glanced in the direction of his truck. "Fine. But the discussion will be about the kids. Can't promise anything else."

Knox shrugged out of his backpack and set it beside me with a heavy *thump*. From his pack he removed the small oxygen tank hooked to my mask and set it in my lap. I expected he'd hold out a hand to help me to my feet or something. Instead, he scooped me up -- oxygen tank and all -- and carried me toward the trailer where the children waited.

"What are you doing?"

"I'm takin' you to the hospital." There was a warning in his voice that said I shouldn't argue. But I didn't think it would be the smartest move to give in to this guy.

"If I need to go to the hospital, I'll go later. I need to take care of my children first."

"Evelyn." Mr. Knoxville was gentle as he adjusted the oxygen mask on my face to free a few strands of hair. "Your lungs were hurt because you inhaled too much smoke. We need to get you checked over to make sure you don't need additional treatment. You know that."

"I'll be fine. And I'm not saying I won't see my doctor, but I need to take care of the kids first. What if they need to see a doctor more than I do? We haven't taken stock of their injuries yet."

"I'm pretty sure there are enough doctors in the city to go around." Knox didn't so much as look at me as he set me down in the cab of the truck. "I vote we take you *all* to the hospital to get checked out." He glanced at Mr. Knoxville. "Including you, old man."

Mr. Knoxville rolled his eyes. "I'm not stupid, boy. I fully intend to get checked out, but you need to keep in mind we thought you were dead. You ain't been here in fifteen years, seven months, and four days. Which means you don't get to dictate to me. Old man or not."

"I think you really should get seen, Mom." Luke ignored the byplay between Mr. Knoxville and his son, focusing instead on me and his sister. "We'll all go and you'll be there with us."

"I'll take you and Aneshya. If I try to get seen too, they might put us in separate rooms. If I still feel bad after you guys are cleared, I'll check in then. OK? Besides, we've still got to find Danny. He was right beside me when we realized there was a fire."

"Fuck him," Luke muttered.

That shocked me. "Luke! Why would you say something like that?"

The kid looked disgruntled and more than a little miserable but shook his head. "Sorry, Mom."

Luke had started calling Danny by his first name a few weeks ago. Both of them refused to tell me why, and if Aneshya knew, she wasn't saying either. Given the fact the poor girl couldn't keep a secret to save her life, I figured she was telling the truth when she told me she didn't know what had happened. But the relationship between Luke and his father had changed. Drastically.

"Mr. Knoxville, I have to find him. Can you take the children to the ER, and I'll meet you there? I need to find Danny, but I don't want to wait to get them care."

"Evie. Honey." Mr. Knoxville sighed, placing a hand on my shoulder before giving it a gentle squeeze. "How many times have I told you to call me Grover?

And yes, Danny is my son, but these are my grandkids. You are the daughter of my heart." He gave Knox a wry smile. "Had you been around when Danny first met Evie, I have no doubt you'd be their protector, Denver."

"Yeah, well, I wasn't. I'm not." Knox frowned, looking like he didn't take too kindly to Mr. Knoxville's words. The last thing I wanted was to be on this guy's bad side, but I wasn't asking for anything from him.

"Danny isn't their protector either. Someone needs to take care of them."

"Don't talk about me like I'm not here, or, worse, like I'm not capable of keeping my children safe." My heart was starting to pound. Anger and fear rose up to overshadow any injuries I had.

"No one's saying you can't take care of Luke and Aneshya." Mr. Knoxville sighed and shook his head. "Danny isn't the right man for you. He's not a good father to those kids, and you know it better than me. You're just too kind to say so."

"Good or bad, he's still their father."

"He's an asshole," Luke muttered.

"Luke!"

"Well, he is, Mom. He's never here. He's always got... other things to take care of," Luke said, not meeting my gaze.

"Honey, your father's a busy man. He works so hard."

Luke snorted. "Yeah. Whatever." Luke looked away but didn't stray far from me or his sister.

"Luke." Knox addressed my son. "Get your sister into the truck. Start it if you need to. I'm gonna secure my gear, then we'll go to the hospital."

"Why won't you guys listen to me?" I would

have screamed if I could have, but it came out more of a croak. "Danny is still in there somewhere!"

"He's not." Mr. Knoxville said, giving Knox a look I couldn't decipher.

"Come on, Mom," Luke said, taking my hand. "Aneshya says her chest hurts. We need to get to the hospital."

I hadn't really noticed but firefighters and police had finally turned up and were fighting the fire and blocking the place off. "Aren't you with the fire department or the ambulance service?" I looked up at Knox who shook his head.

"No." No other explanation. How the hell did he have all this equipment if he wasn't with fire or EMS? "Come on. We need to get going."

Mr. Knoxville was already in the truck with the kids. Surprisingly, he'd started the vehicle before climbing in the back with them. Luke was fussing over Aneshya while Mr. Knoxville sat staring out the window at the burning building.

"I'm sure he got out, Mr. Knoxville."

The older man sighed before turning to face me. "Evelyn, I'm not going to tell you again. You'll call me Grover. You call me *mister* anything again, I'll put you over my knee."

That got a giggle from Aneshya. I glanced back at her. She had covered her mouth with her hand, and Luke was trying to smother a grin.

"I suppose that means he told you." Knox had opened the door and was climbing inside the cab. "Put that oxygen mask back on..." He glanced back at my children before adding, "young lady."

That got another giggle from Aneshya. Knox, though as scary a man as I'd ever seen, glanced back at my daughter and... *winked.*

Sweet God…

With that gleam of humor and the upward twitch of his lips, Knox was… devastating. It was only a glimpse before his mask of indifference was back, but I knew without a doubt he'd shown that side of himself to the children to ease their fears. Aneshya wasn't immune to his charm, though Luke just sneered at him. That was my son. If it involved me or his sister, he wasn't prepared to take anything at face value.

By the time we pulled up outside the Emergency Room, I was crashing. Hard. The adrenaline had left my system, and I shivered uncontrollably. The big man beside me put his truck in park, then reached over and engulfed my hand in his much bigger one. "It's gonna be all right. You're safe."

The kindness in his eyes… The concern. He looked at me like I'd wanted Danny to look at me during our entire years-long relationship. Perhaps he had looked at me that way once. Maybe when the kids had been born. All I knew for sure was, if Knox kept looking at me this way, that look would be my undoing.

Chapter Two

Knox

I was never supposed to reveal my presence to my family. It was something I'd agreed to when things went to shit with my last mission and I'd wanted out. Instead of giving me a new identity or some shit like that, I opted to be dead and let my father collect benefits on me. But with all the things that had happened recently, with our vice president keeping in touch with her family and insisting family was everything, I'd realized how much I'd missed mine. I knew it would be hard and that contacting him was a risk, but I had to see my father. Of all the people in my life, I knew he'd understand. And that was where I intended to leave my reunion. Only with my dad. What I wasn't prepared for was my brother's woman.

Sure, I'd seen her from afar as I'd scouted out the apartment where my dad lived. Watched as she took the kids to school. Picked them up. Took them to school functions and sporting activities. My dad usually went with her because Danny was never there. I'd actually thought Crush and Byte had been mistaken and Danny wasn't living in the same apartment. That was how rarely I'd seen him.

My nephew, Luke, was an avid football player, while Aneshya was more into music and dancing. From what I'd been able to piece together over the past six months, Evelyn was doing her level best to be a good mother. She had a job where she worked from home and, from what Crush had told me, she took care of every single bill the small family had. Danny took care of himself. I hadn't been that interested in learning about Danny. The two of us had never really gotten along, despite being raised in the same household. We couldn't be more different. Besides, it was Danny's spending and lavish lifestyle that had forced me into the special forces to begin with.

He'd managed to take out multiple loans on our parents' home and property he either couldn't or wouldn't pay back. Mom and Dad didn't have that kind of money and couldn't even meet the monthly interest payments. I'd tried, but no matter how much money I sent, Danny managed to end up with more than half of it. Which had led to a whole other chain of events which led me to being declared dead. My pension and death benefits were enough to pay off the lien, but I had no idea why Dad was living in the same apartment complex as Danny and Evelyn instead of his home. I knew Dad had moved out shortly after my mother had passed, so I'd made sure the guy he hired to keep up the property did so, and I took over paying him.

Once at the hospital, my dad corralled the kids, making sure they got signed in. Evelyn worried her bottom lip nervously. She didn't have her purse or wallet, so I was sure she didn't have her insurance card with her. If she even had any.

We got everyone checked in and into triage. The kids seemed to be doing far better once they'd gotten into the clear air, but I was worried about Evelyn. Her voice was husky and she still coughed a lot, though she didn't seem to be having as much trouble as before.

"I'm fine," she insisted after the nurse listened to her chest. "I really don't need to be seen. Just see the kids and Mr. -- uh" -- she glanced at my dad --"that is, Grover and the kids. See to them."

The nurse gave her a look. "Honey, of the four of you, you need to be seen the worst. Your lungs sound awful, your oxygen is low, and your voice is hoarse."

"She'll be seen." There was no way I was letting her sit this one out.

She looked up at me. "I can't afford this," she hissed. "The kids? Yes. Me? I'll be fine."

"Yep," I agreed, nodding my head. "'Cause you're gonna let the doc check you out."

"We've got several people coming in from the fire, honey. Of all the ones I've seen here in triage so far, you're by far the one hurt the worst. If it's the money you're worried about, don't. We'll see you regardless. You'll still get a bill and stuff, but you can pay it off a few dollars at a time."

"She's good." And she would be. Because I knew I wouldn't let her be anything but.

"I still don't think it's necessary. I'll be fine. I'm already much better."

"It is. Now stop arguing." I gave her a steady look, expecting her to wilt and comply with my orders. Most everyone did.

"You can't tell me what to do." Her eyes flashed and she stuck her chin up. She looked like she was as big a warrior as my vice president... Right up until her lungs spasmed and she started coughing uncontrollably for a full minute.

The nurse waited patiently, rubbing her back after putting an oxygen mask on her. When Evelyn finally stopped coughing, the nurse raised an eyebrow. "Honey, I think he already did. And you just proved his point."

Poor Evelyn looked like she was going to cry. Which made my chest decidedly uncomfortable. Then a thought occurred to me. "Get Dr. Benedict. Tell him Knox is here."

The nurse hesitated a moment before giving me a little frown. Not like she was displeased. More like I was someone who didn't understand how this whole hospital and doctor-in-the-wrong-department thing worked. "I'll shoot him a text, but you know Dr. Benedict doesn't work the ER. Right?"

"Understood. I'll call him."

The nurse shrugged before gathering up everything she needed. "Wait here and I'll get a wheelchair for you. I think everyone else is good to walk?" She looked up at my father with a questioning eye. As I expected, my father snorted.

"Why wouldn't I be fine to walk? Been walkin' for over seventy years."

She smiled. "Figured as much, Mr. Knoxville."

My dad scowled. "If I get mistered one more time…"

The nurse gave my father a smirk. "Feisty. Good. Means you're OK."

"Just take us back," I muttered. "I'll carry her."

"I can walk." Evelyn's voice was still hoarse, and I could hear her wheezing easily.

"Sure, you can. Still ain't gonna." I didn't look at her because I wasn't sure I could keep from making a fool of myself if I did. This was my brother's woman. She'd had his children. If ever there was a woman who was off-limits, it was this one. Even if Danny wasn't there to help her or married to her, she was still his woman.

Either she was tired of arguing or she was starting to feel the effects of smoke inhalation, because she settled passively in my arms as I carried her down the hallway to the room the nurse led us to.

No sooner had I set her on the bed than Bullet walked in. I hadn't had time to call him, so the nurse must have texted him.

"You know, I could have done without you

turning up on my last official day at the hospital, Knox." Bullet scowled, but it was directed at me. The second he shifted to look at everyone else in the room, his expression changed to something warm and inviting. "I'm Dr. Benedict. I hear you've all had quite the adventure today."

It was the girl, Aneshya, who spoke up. "The building caught on fire. He saved us." She pointed at me.

"Well, Knox is good for stuff like that. Do you guys care if I look you over?"

Bullet glanced at the monitor that showed Evelyn's vital signs and heart rhythm before turning his attention to the other three. He took his time listening to the kids and Dad. While that was happening, nurses and other technicians came in and started IVs and took blood from Evelyn. She protested, but Dad put his hand on her shoulder and squeezed.

"For me, Evie," he murmured. "For the kids."

With a sigh, she stilled and let everyone continue to poke and prod her. Luke had her hand as well as Aneshya's, holding on tightly. It was clear the young man was protective of the women in his life. Unlike his father.

"I think you three are fine," Bullet said with a grin at Luke and Aneshya. "I'd like to get a chest X-ray for all three of you, though. Just to be on the safe side. Especially for you, Grover." Bullet gave Dad a smug look. The older man grunted at him. Obviously, Bullet had been clued into the fact Dad didn't like formalities. "You're obviously fit and in great health, but you're still more susceptible to the effects of smoke inhalation than everyone else here. Like it or not, you're still an old fart."

That got a bark of laughter from my dad.

"Damned straight. I earned that status a long time ago."

"As for you…" Bullet turned to address Evelyn. "Plan on being here a while."

"I'm fine." Her little croak did nothing to solidify her declaration.

Bullet tapped the tablet he held in his hands. "The first tests coming back say otherwise. I'll hold my final judgment until everything is complete, but you're going to let me do several more tests, give you some medicine, some nebulizer treatments, and all kinds of medical things." He grinned at her, and I wanted to punch my friend. When Bullet raised an eyebrow at me, I realized I'd been growling. "My. Someone's in a snit."

"She's my brother's woman, so she's taken."

"Got my own woman, brother. Two is more than I can handle." He winked at Evelyn before leaving.

"Do we have another uncle we've never met?" Luke scowled at me, then my dad.

"No, Luke," My dad scrubbed a hand over his face. "I'm pretty sure he means 'brother' in a different way."

"I know… uh… Dr. Benedict from my time in the service." Not a lie. I'd met Bullet when my team had come back shot all to hell. He'd saved my life.

"Oh. So he's like a *friend* brother." Luke nodded like he got it.

"I suppose you could say that. Yeah. But more."

"'Cause you've been through stuff together." Maybe the kid did understand.

A woman came to take Evelyn for a test. When they'd left, Luke looked back at me. "Will Dr. Benedict take care of my mom?"

"If your mother is hurt, he'll find out how sick

she is and know how to fix it."

Luke looked to his grandfather for reassurance. When my dad nodded his head, I felt more gratitude than I ever thought possible. I was beyond needing my dad's approval for anything. The fact was, I'd left him. And Mom. I'd given him no reason to believe in me, but he did.

We waited mostly in silence while the techs and nurses did tests and gave medicines to Evelyn. Dad and the kids each got nebulizer treatments and some steroids, but Bullet proclaimed them and my dad otherwise unharmed. Evelyn, he wanted to admit, but she refused.

"I'll take medicine or whatever, but I can't stay." She was firm, even though her voice was still hoarse. I could still hear her wheezing, but she did seem a bit stronger. "I've got to take care of my family."

"I can look after Luke and Aneshya," Dad said, speaking gently to Evelyn. "You can't take care of them if you're injured. Let Dr. Benedict keep you to make sure your lungs heal properly."

"No, Mr. Knoxville. I'm going home with my children."

"Home to where?" The question popped out before I could stop myself. "Your place is gone. Burnt to the fuckin' ground along with anything you owned inside that fuckin' building. Where you gonna go?"

"Knox." Dad stood, placing himself between me and Evelyn. I wanted to shove him out of the way, but I had no right. Besides, he was protecting Evelyn. Right now, he was protecting her from me.

Aneshya gasped, reaching for her brother who pulled her into his arms. The young man glared at me. "You're just like your brother," he muttered.

"No, Luke." Dad didn't take his eyes off me as he

spoke to the boy. "He's not. He's trying to force the issue because he knows it's what's best for your mother. Knox is used to having any orders he gives obeyed."

"That doesn't mean he can be mean to my mom or upset my sister."

"Fuck," I muttered. "I ain't good at this."

"No." Luke gave me a look few men I knew had ever dared give me. He was angry, and I was the cause of his anger. "You're not."

"We can all stay at my house outside Riviera Beach." Dad squeezed my shoulder before turning to Luke and Aneshya, kneeling down in front of them. "It's been closed up for several years so we'll have to get a few things to make it livable, but I think we can find what we need easily enough."

"I'll help." I needed to make things right. "I'm sorry, Luke. Aneshya. I only want what's best for your mother."

"I can take care of myself." Evelyn spoke so softly I almost didn't hear her. When I turned my gaze to her, she ducked her head, her hands bunched in the blanket draped over her lap.

"You can. But everyone needs help sometimes. Now, it's your turn. I'll get some friends to help open up the house. I'll see what everyone needs and have it delivered. In the meantime, you should strongly consider doing as Dr. Benedict told you. Stay here. Get IV antibiotics and steroids. Maybe you'll be fine, and we can bring you home tomorrow."

"I can't leave my kids. They've been through something horrifying. They need me."

"We'll be fine, Mom." Luke stood and took his mother's hand. "I'll look after Aneshya and Grandpa. If they need help, I'll make sure they get it."

"Honey, this isn't your job."

"I'm not a kid, Mom. Besides, I can do a much better job than Danny."

Evelyn was silent for a long time, holding her son's hand and rubbing the back of it gently. "You know he hates it when you call him by his first name."

"Well, I ain't callin' him Dad."

"I'll tell Bullet you're stayin'," I said, taking out my phone.

"Who's Bullet?" Luke asked, turning his head sharply in my direction.

"Sorry. Dr. Benedict. Bullet is, er, was his call sign. It's how I've always known him."

"And he's a doctor." I had to give Luke credit. The kid didn't back down. He was demanding when it came to the people around his family. Kid was an alpha male in the making. "Named Bullet? Isn't that like an oxymoron or something?"

I shrugged. "I didn't give him the name. You'll have to ask him."

"Ask me what?" Bullet stepped into the room, a grin on his face.

"How'd you get the name Bullet?"

He shrugged. "Lots of reasons a person gets a name. It was the military." He focused on Evelyn. "Now. I get why you don't want to stay. I also happen to know Knox here has some medical supplies at his disposal, including oxygen if you need it. So, if you agree to let him stay with you, I'll let you go home. Otherwise, you'll stay here."

"You can't force me to stay. I'll sign out against advice. Isn't that what people do?"

He nodded. "Yeah, but I have the feeling I can get through to your son, and he'll persuade you to stay."

"You'd use my kids against me." It wasn't a question, and I wasn't sure I liked how she teared up.

"Honey, I'm a doctor. I'll do everything in my power to help someone who needs it. And you need it. So, if you won't let Knox stay with you, I'll have to get Luke here to guilt you into staying." He shook his head, crossing his arms over his chest. "No one wants that, Evelyn."

"Knox probably has other things to do." She gripped Luke's hand harder, and the young man, bless his heart, gripped her hands in both of his.

"Sure. I've got to spend time with my father. Fortunately, you're staying with my father, too. Win-win." I tried to give her an encouraging smile but wasn't sure I managed it. Mostly because I was way happier about that particular situation than I should be. It was a very uncomfortable feeling.

"Good," my dad said, rubbing his hands together. "We can take our Evie home and be sure she has everything she needs."

Bullet gave a crisp nod. "Good. I'll go get her discharge instructions and scripts ready. Knox, you need anything, you let me know. I'll make sure you have it."

"I'll need another oxygen tank. Used most of what I had in the trailer. Albuterol and Atrovent too. Or anything else you think she needs."

"No problem. I'll text the guys. They helpin' get you relocated?"

"Haven't asked yet, but that's the plan."

"I'll give 'em a heads-up. Give me the address and someone'll be there soon."

I held out my hand to Bullet. "Thanks, man. I owe you."

Bullet jerked his head toward Evelyn and the

kids. "Take care of them. That's payment enough."

A few minutes later and four hours after we first got to the hospital, after the nurse had given me a packet of papers for everyone, we started out of the ER. I carried Evelyn while the kids and my father walked with us.

"I'm perfectly capable of walking," Evelyn protested as we left the room. She didn't struggle to get down, though. Which told me everything I needed to know. She was still weak. Probably exhausted. She smelled like smoke and old burning building, but underneath that was a sweetness I tried hard to ignore. She was my brother's woman. I'd thought it earlier, but I had to keep reminding myself just how the fuck off-limits she was.

Just before we rounded the corner Aneshya sucked in a breath before running ahead. "Daddy!" Sure enough, in the room in front of us Danny sat at the bedside of a very pregnant woman. She scowled as Aneshya threw herself into Danny's arms, hugging him tightly. "We were so worried! Mommy made us leave the building, but she tried to find you. Grandpa and Mr. Knox pulled her out, but the smoke made her sick."

Danny didn't push her away, but he didn't hug the child either. When he looked up and saw me, his eyes widened. He did push his daughter away this time, his gaze taking in the rest of us. His gaze rested on Evelyn before returning to me again.

"Denver. Holy shit."

"Knox," I corrected. "I go by Knox now."

"Where you been, man? We thought you were dead."

"Long story." I nodded to the woman in the bed. "Guessing you've got a long story as well."

"Who are these people, Danny?"

"No one, honey. Don't worry about them. We need to make sure you and the baby are OK." Did he honestly think he was going to get anyone to just ignore this whole thing? His woman would ignore all of us? And that his kids weren't going to understand what was happening? Hell. Did he even care about any of us, especially his kids?

Luke tugged at his sister's hand, pulling her away from my brother. "Come on, Aneshya." He gave Danny a disgusted look. "We're leaving."

I still carried Evelyn. She was trembling in my arms. Danny hadn't even acknowledged her. As she looked from the woman in the bed to Danny and back, her breathing quickened.

"Calm down, Evelyn." I tried to speak calmly when I wanted to set her down and pound the living hell outta my brother. "You want to go home. And you can't do that if you have a panic attack on the way out the door." She nodded. "Put your arms around my neck and put your face against my shoulder," I whispered. "Not a sound until we're out of here. You can do it."

My dad ushered the kids out. "Take them to the truck, Knox. I'll be there in a minute."

"If you're telling Danny to go to hell, I wanna stay." Luke lifted his chin, glaring daggers at my brother. Seems he was good to let his sister go with me so he could stay and see his own father get a dressing down. I understood him completely.

Danny just sat there. I recognized the look on his face from years past. He knew he was in trouble and was going to sit there and take it. Then he'd continue on like nothing happened. The question was, would he want to stay in Evelyn's and his children's lives, or stay with his new woman.

"Why is she calling you Daddy?" The woman gave my brother a look somewhere between anger and anguish.

"Because Danny's her father." My dad might be over seventy, but he was still in top physical condition and he wasn't a small man. He could intimidate better than almost anyone I knew. Well, except possibly Lemon. But in my defense, any woman who refused to clean the blood off herself after she helped beat men to a bloody pulp just so she could get one over on the club girls in Grim Road deserved to be feared. "It's obvious to me you're as innocent as Evelyn in this, so I'm sorry to tell you Danny has two children with Evelyn."

"Well, I'm sorry to tell you he's my husband. We've been married for fifteen years." Her voice shook, and I knew she was on the verge of tears. "I never thought I'd be able to have kids, so this is our first child." She turned accusing eyes to Danny. "What's going on?"

"He's just a crazy old man, honey. Those kids are my brother's."

"Then why did the girl call *you* Daddy? And why have I never heard about your brother? Or your father? You told me all your family was dead!"

"You were always your mother's favorite, Danny." My father looked angrier than I could ever remember seeing him. "But she'd be ashamed of you if she were still alive."

"So your mother really is dead?" The woman looked like she was simultaneously on the verge of tears and tearing Danny's heart out with her bare hands. "I guess that's one thing you told the truth about."

"Honey, I --"

"Save it," she bit out. "I can't think about this right now." She rubbed her tummy, obviously comforting herself. This woman was as much a victim as Evelyn. Maybe more. Evelyn hadn't moved once she'd tucked her face against my shoulder.

"Knox." Dad lifted an eyebrow at me. "Remove them from this situation. Please." He asked nicely, but it was a clear order from a man who expected to be obeyed.

I nodded my head. "Luke. Aneshya. Let's get your mom in the truck and settled. Then we'll all go... home."

"I want to hear what Grandpa has to say to Danny," Luke said stubbornly.

"I know you do. But your mom needs you right now. Both of you."

"She needs Grandpa too," Aneshya said softly, obviously confused and not sure what to think. If she'd put it together, I couldn't tell, but Luke certainly had. I'd bet my left nut the kid knew his dad had another woman before we'd seen the proof. And it sounded that, though he had two kids by Evelyn, she was the side piece. Not this woman.

No matter what happened next, this wasn't going to end well. "Come on, Dad. It's done. Let it go for now. Evelyn needs us all."

Dad lifted an eyebrow. "Us? So you're part of this family now?" Yeah. Dad was good and pissed. Which meant no one in the wrong was going to get off easy. That included me.

"I have a good reason. Which I'll happily tell you. *Later.*"

"Fine," he grumbled. "You're right." He turned back to Danny. "You need to be prepared to give us all an explanation."

"I don't have to tell you nothin', old man."

My father took two steps toward Danny, then he backhanded him. "You've disrespected me for the last time," he snarled. "Do not come home unless you're prepared to tell me what the fuck is goin' on, son. You do, there'll be more where that came from."

"Everything all right here?"

Shit. Two nurses stood in the doorway. Likely, they'd either seen or heard my dad hit Danny.

"Yeah. Everything's fine." Danny glared at my dad but turned away when Dad stared him down.

"We were just leaving." Dad took Aneshya's hand and gently guided her to the door. Luke lingered behind.

"You're not our father anymore." He lifted his chin. "Don't bother my mom. You do, I'll kill you."

Danny didn't say anything. Hell, he couldn't even look Luke in the eyes. To his credit, Luke never wavered. He stood there until Danny finally looked up, acknowledging his son. Then Luke turned and walked out the door, following his grandfather and sister. I brought up the rear with a trembling Evelyn in my arms. That was the moment I decided they were all mine. I'd take care of them. I'd protect them. And if Danny showed his fuckin' head anywhere near any of them ever again, Luke wouldn't have to kill him. I would.

Chapter Three

Evelyn

I didn't know what to think. I guess somewhere deep inside me that I'd never acknowledged existed, I knew Danny had something going on. Granted, I wasn't expecting this. But it actually made sense in a way.

"Danny moved in with me right before I found out I was pregnant with Luke," I murmured. I wasn't certain who I was talking to. Musing to myself out loud, I guess. We were in Knox's truck, headed to Mr. Knoxville's house. I'd never known he'd had an actual house. Why was he living in that apartment if he had a perfectly good house? "I guess I just got so used to him being with me I never wondered why we hadn't gotten married." I sniffed. "I mean, I guess I should have known. Looking back, he was only home about half the week. Sometimes longer. Sometimes he'd be gone for a couple weeks or more at a time. You know. For work." I sounded like I was in shock. I suppose I was.

"Honey, there's gonna be plenty of time to sort this all out." Mr. Knoxville gripped my shoulder from where he sat in the back seat. Grover. I had to start thinking of him as Grover. If I pissed him off, he might not let me stay with him, and I had nowhere else to go. What if he decided he wanted to take my children? I mean, they were his grandchildren, and he was the one who could give them a roof over their heads and a safe place to stay.

"No one's gonna take your children, Evelyn."

"Not on your life!"

Both men spoke over top of each other. Vehemently.

Had I said that out loud?

"Mom?" Aneshya sounded confused and scared. I knew Luke was angry. Me? I didn't know what to do. What to think.

"She's in shock." Knox reached over and took my hand, gripping it tightly. He'd put me in the front seat with him. Even fastened my seat belt for me.

"Just get us home," Grover ordered. "She needs to clean up and then rest. She'll feel much better then."

"Who's gonna try to take us from Mommy?"

"No one, Aneshya. I won't let anyone take us from Mom. Don't worry." Luke sounded confident and determined.

I needed to pull myself together. I was scaring my children. Hell, I was scaring myself.

"I will never let anyone take you away from your mother, Aneshya." I thought that came from Knox. When I looked over at him, his free hand gripped the wheel. His jaw was clenched. He still had my hand firmly in his. For some reason, even though he was talking to my daughter, I believed Knox. It settled me when I had no reason to believe him. I didn't know this man.

But he'd saved us. He'd saved us, then took care of us.

"Just relax. You'll feel better when you've rested and had time to process."

I snorted a laugh. "Yeah. Process. This is all… too damned much!"

"I know." Grover muttered. "We're almost home, honey."

"How could he do this? How could I not know he had another woman?"

"Not your fault, honey. I'm his father and I didn't know either."

"I knew." Luke's muttered confession startled

me. I looked back at him, my mouth open in shock.

"What?"

"I saw him. With her. She lives in the penthouse." Luke turned to face the window. "A month ago."

That made sense. That was about the time Luke started calling his father *Danny*. It was also when he became super protective of both me and his sister. He'd been leaning that way, but something pushed him over the top.

Knox pulled into the driveway of a ranch-style home. It had an upstairs, but Grover said that was mostly attic space. It was surprisingly well-kept considering no one had lived here for several years, if I'd understood Grover right. It didn't exactly look lived in, at least from the outside, but the yard was well-kept as was the outside of the house. There were no special touches, though. No flowers in the yard. No outside furniture on the porch. No trash bins.

"I haven't been here in years," Grover murmured. "Still looks like the last day I saw it." He took in a shuddering breath. "I paid someone to keep the place up because I just couldn't. Funny. Until this moment, I hadn't realized I haven't gotten a bill from the guy I hired. I... tried to push the place out of my mind. Too damned many memories."

"I made sure your guy kept the place up." Knox turned off the engine. "Kept the yard mowed and made sure the place wasn't looted or had squatters living there, but the inside is pretty bare." About that time, a moving van pulled up along with another big F-150 like Knox's, only this one was white where Knox's was black. "Which we're fixing to remedy now."

He opened the door and everyone else followed.

I fumbled with my seat belt, finally getting it undone when Knox opened my door.

"Out you get, little one."

When he pulled me into his arms to carry me, I tried to protest. "I'm OK to walk." It was more a reflex than something I truly thought I was capable of doing. I was used to shrugging off my weaknesses and simply powering through.

"Yeah? Maybe I'm not ready to let you walk." Knox cradled me against him. God, it felt good! This man, someone I didn't know, made me feel safe and more cared for than Danny had the entire thirteen years we'd been together. Tears were very, very close. Though not for the reasons I expected. They were more for the tenderness being shown to me by everyone involved than Danny's betrayal. Which told me everything I needed to know about my relationship with Danny.

"Don't do this." I whispered my plea, half hoping he hadn't heard me. The other half knew letting him care for me was a really bad idea.

"Don't do what?" Knox carried me inside the house like I weighed nothing. It was like something out of a fairy tale. Except that his face was an emotionless mask and he didn't look at me.

"Take care of me. I'll get used to it and..."

He just grunted and carried me to the bathroom. "Your room and the kids' both attach to this bathroom." He pointed out two doors on either side. "Go ahead and get in the shower. I'll bring you a change of clothes and some towels."

"I don't have any clothes." I whispered. "The fire..."

"I've got that taken care of. If you can give me a couple minutes, I'll bring in your toiletries. Then you can get the soot and smoke off you. By that time, I should have a bed set up for you and you can lie down."

"But the children --"

"-- are doing the same thing." Knox set me on the vanity before gripping my shoulders in a firm but gentle grip. "I'll look after the kids and my dad. Though, I think Luke has both of them under control. He's a very protective kid."

"He's always been like that, but the last month? Yeah. When he said he'd seen Danny with that woman a month ago, I realized that's when he started to really assume the role of man of the house."

"Yeah. I get that." He sighed, looking away. "Look. You're safe. I'll take care of everything."

"I don't know you." I had no idea why I was protesting when I really needed someone to take over, even if it was just for a few hours so I could process. Honestly, though, I wasn't sure much was going to change. Other than Danny would no longer make his occasional appearance.

"No. But I helped get you out of a burning building. Give me the benefit of the doubt. I'm not gonna hurt you, Evelyn." He sounded so sincere I wanted to believe him. I was so confused right now! All I wanted to do was huddle in the corner with my children and lick my wounds for a few hours.

"There are other ways of hurting someone than just physically," I whispered.

"I know. Ain't gonna do that either." He held my gaze for long moments. Then he gave me a crisp nod and helped me off the counter to my feet. "I'll be right back. You can clean up, and I'll get us all some supper." I'd been in the middle of fixing lunch when the fire alarm had started blaring. I suppose it was time for supper.

There was nothing else to say or do. I just nodded, knowing he was right. Besides, I'd be more able to process and think once I was clean, full, and rested. I would figure out what to do from here on. Right now, I wanted to shut down. Let someone else take control. After that, I'd start evaluating the pieces of my life and how to proceed.

Chapter Four

Knox

Evelyn rested the rest of the day, for which I felt more relief than I had a right to. She should have stayed in the hospital, but I didn't have the right to push that kind of care on her. The kids seemed to adjust quickly. Aneshya was upset the day immediately after the fire, but it seemed to be more that she'd lost some things important to her than missing her father. It was puzzling. I knew they had a very relaxed relationship, but I had no idea it was this spartan.

"Danny's never home." Dad stood beside me. Lemon, Apple and Cecelia had showed up too, keeping Evelyn company while Luke, Aneshya, and a girl of nine or ten named Effie play in the backyard. A week had passed, and the kids were acting like normal kids. Well, except for Luke, who was twelve going on forty. "He'd show up from time to time, giving Evie and the kids some excuse about how he had to travel for work but never brought home money. He never took care of them. Everything the kids have, Evelyn provided. Even the apartment was paid for by her."

"What the fuck was my brother doing?" It was more a musing than a question I expected an actual answer to. My brother had always been a selfish bastard, but this was next level.

"I'll be honest, Knox. I've worried over Danny since before you disappeared."

"You and Mom both. He was always into something… expensive."

Dad snorted. "No shit. The woman he was with at the hospital, the woman who claims to be his wife of fifteen years? She owns the building. I've seen her there, but she didn't really pay attention to the people around her." He shook his head. "We're all kind of beneath her notice. Probably how Danny was able to live a double life so effectively with the mother of his children being in the same building."

"Evelyn was too busy trying to keep a roof over her family's head and food on the table to question him much. His actual wife couldn't imagine he'd have an affair with a woman she sees as second-class compared to both of them."

"Yep. I'm not sure what Danny's goal was, but my guess is he's lost both women."

"You heard from him?"

I barked out a laugh. "No. Doubt I will, even if he knew how to contact me. I figured you'd be the one he'd reach out to."

"No. Danny and I haven't seen eye to eye in several years. I thought he was just a workaholic. Until I found out Evie had been the one paying all the bills. Making sure the kids got to their extracurricular activities. She was basically a single mom with Danny poking his head in every now and then to say hello. You notice how Aneshya shrugged off not having her dad here after we all moved?"

"Yeah. They're not used to him being here, so they don't miss him in their lives that much." The more I learned about everything going on, the less I liked it.

"What about you?"

My dad glanced at me sharply. "What about me?"

"You got my pension. Death benefits. All my personal possessions. Why did you make it look like you'd sold this place? Why move to that apartment building?"

"I moved there to protect my family. Because, at

the time, the memories here were too much." There was a pause as he cleared his throat before he continued. "And…" He scrubbed a hand over his face with a sigh. "Because Danny was going through money like hell wouldn't have it. After he took out all those loans on the house and property, once I got them all paid off with your death benefits, I told him I'd sold the house. That I was broke. All I had was my social security check. He didn't know about anything I got from you. I've been putting all that into savings for the kids. Figured they'd need something for college or whatever they wanted to do after high school. I keep the fridge and cupboards stocked with food. Evelyn pretends not to notice, but she always has me over for dinner and makes reheatable breakfasts and lunches for me. She also cleans my apartment when I'm not looking." He sounded and looked disgruntled, but I saw the affection he had for Evelyn. I figured he let her because my dad knew Evelyn wouldn't want him doing so much for her without her repaying him. Since she was on a limited budget, that was how she did it. "Hadn't expected you to have me listed as an actual dependent and not just a beneficiary, though. How'd you make that happen?"

"It wasn't easy, believe me. I had to pull some strings and threaten more than a few bureaucrats to make it happen. But when I heard you'd moved out of the house, I figured Danny was up to his old shit."

"Danny never stopped his old shit. I think he spends everything he makes. Well, that's assuming he even had some kind of job. He was pretty good at moving around the building without being seen where he wasn't supposed to be. My guess is he's mooching off his wife's bank account and either stays in the penthouse with her or in Evelyn's apartment. I doubt he's ever had a serious job."

"How the hell did he keep all this secret? I had the best people I know looking into you and never once did they turn up that Danny was married."

"Good Goddamn question. I lived next door to the kid for over a decade and had no fuckin' clue, Knox." Dad shook his head slightly. I knew the feeling, and I wasn't as close to Danny as our father was. "Makes me wonder what else he has going on."

"What happens now?" I asked the question, but I knew. No way Danny stayed away too long.

Dad crossed his hands over his chest. "Don't give a fuck. Figured we'll find out the second Danny turns up. And he *will* turn up."

"Wanting money."

"Oh, it won't be as obvious as that. He'll worm his way in, making everyone feel sorry for him. Like he's the victim who's being kept from his children. He'll apologize and tell Evelyn how much he loves her. He'll pretend to be involved with his kids, but all the while he'll be scheming and planning the next big thing. And siphoning Evelyn's bank account if she's not careful."

"What?" I barked out the question harsher than I'd meant to. I'd been going with the ebb and flow of the conversation, but I hadn't been expecting that.

"Oh, I think you heard me, Knox. Last time Danny spent any quality time with Evelyn, when he left to go on a 'business trip,' she didn't have money to buy groceries. She spent three hours on the phone with the bank trying to figure out what had happened. There was a five-hundred-dollar ATM withdrawal she swore she didn't make. Her PIN number was used, so she couldn't get the money back. I'm positive it was Danny's doing."

"That fucker left her without a way to care for herself or her children? Is that what you're tellin' me?"

"Yeah, Knox. That's exactly what he did. Evie would never say, but I'm pretty sure that wasn't the first time. That's when I started keeping an eye on her food supply and making sure she was stocked."

"Danny takin' her money stops now."

"Yeah?" Dad turned to me, raising an eyebrow. "How you gonna enforce that?"

"By keepin' Danny away from her."

"Easier said than done. Asshole or not, Danny's still those kids' father."

I sighed. "Yeah. Huge-ass problem there." I had an idea about that, but I'd have to involve Grim Road even more than I already had. I suppose it was time to test Lemon's claim that we always took care of family.

Luke, Aneshya, and Effie were having a ball playing with the stuff Lemon and the girls brought over. Somewhere, she'd managed to score a set of Yard Darts that had to be at least forty years old. Lemon, Apple, and Cecilia were all sitting with Evelyn, chatting away and keeping a close eye on the kids playing with lethal weapons but otherwise didn't seem concerned.

Evelyn flicked her gaze in my direction before ducking her head. She glanced up at me a couple times before turning away and watching the kids again. All the while, the other women kept a running conversation going. Evelyn smiled and nodded in the appropriate places, but I could tell her heart wasn't in it. Every once in a while, her gaze would meet mine, but she never tried to maintain it.

"She's interested in you, Knox." My dad spoke softly. I glanced in his direction briefly to find him smiling.

"She's keeping an eye on the strange man who claims to be her lover's brother. She doesn't know me. She's afraid of me."

"She's afraid of liking you. I've seen her watching you when she thinks you're not looking."

"Probably because I look exactly like Danny, and it's freaking her out."

Dad snorted. "Only twice as big."

"You're proving my point, old man."

"Maybe. But that woman is still interested whether she thinks it's a good idea or not." Dad grabbed my shoulder and squeezed. "Look. I've gotten close to Evie over the years. She's a good woman. An even better mother. I'm not saying you should do anything you don't want to do, but I think you're interested in her too."

"Dad, I've known her for a solid week. Most of that I've spent watching from a distance. Besides, I have no idea how long I'll be able to be in her life. I'm still a soldier. I have to leave the country when we have a job. Which is all something I can't talk about. But she'd be trading one absent man for another, and I'd never do that to her."

"So? Quit. Simple."

"Dad --"

"I'm serious, Knox. I have no idea what you've been doing the last fourteen years, but you're back now. We're all your family, Evie included. A man --"

"-- takes care of his family." I repeated the words with him. It was something Dad had drilled into me and Danny growing up. I'd taken it to heart. My brother… hadn't. "I get it, Dad. But there are things you don't know that I can't explain. I'm back now. But I'm not exactly in a position to quit. When I disappeared, when I *died*, that put me in the lifer category with what I do. I'm only here now because we've had some changes recently in our... dynamics. I had to cut ties with you and Danny, but I did my best to make sure you had everything you needed."

"Did you know about Evelyn?"

I winced and shrugged. "I knew *of* her. Knew she was living with Danny and that they had two kids. Didn't want to look too closely at anyone because it only made me want to come home that much more." I turned to meet my dad's gaze head-on. "I'm sorry I wasn't there when Mom died."

"I basically lost you and Elinor at the same time." I'd never seen my dad show strong emotion before. Now, I'd seen it twice. Anger at my brother when he backhanded the younger man at the hospital. Now, a deep, abiding sorrow. His eyes glistened, but he didn't let the tears fall, blinking them back. "We both knew why you went into the military. You sent us most of your pay every month. You knew Danny was bleeding us dry, and you fixed the problem the best way you knew how."

"No, I didn't. Shoulda killed him. That might have pissed off Mom, but it would have kept him from taking advantage of you guys."

"Your mother would never have forgiven you if you had." He gave me a steady look. Mom might not have, but he would've.

I snorted. "Yeah, she would've. Maybe not for a long time, but she would've."

"After she turned you into the authorities herself? Sure." Dad grinned. "She'd have even come to visit you in prison every weekend and Thanksgiving, Christmas, and maybe even Easter."

"Easter is always on a weekend."

Dad shrugged. "Easter too, then."

We held each other's gaze for several seconds before we both broke down and chuckled. Yeah. Mom would have forgiven me, but she'd have seen to it I paid for my crimes. And never looked at me the same way again. Just like with Danny. We might do things she morally objected to with everything in her being, but we were still her sons.

"Elinor would be proud of the man you've become, Knox." He grinned. "She'd call you Denver, though. Not Knox."

"Why the fuck did she name me after a fuckin' city in Colorado?"

Dad really did laugh then. "She didn't and you know it."

"I never liked her brother, you know."

"She didn't either."

"Then why --"

"Because he was her baby brother. She'd promised him when she and I got married that she'd name her firstborn after him."

"And Mom never went back on her word."

"Exactly."

I turned back to the yard. And Evelyn. She was so beautiful and caring I couldn't wrap my mind around how my brother had treated her so badly. Or why she'd put up with him treating her that way.

Dad and I stood in companionable silence for a long time. Finally, I spoke, not looking at my father. "She'd have called me Knox."

"She'd have called you Knox."

Chapter Five

Evelyn

"Guys, time for school." I'd fixed breakfast and the kids had eaten, but now they were dragging their feet getting out the door to the bus stop. It was at the end of the road, so I usually walked with them.

"Coming, Mom." Aneshya was always the one ready to go, but she showed solidarity with her brother by not coming out to leave before he did. Luke was on a mission to home school, so he could stay here and take care of me and his grandfather. Which wasn't happening.

"Lunches are on the counter."

Five minutes later, both Luke and Aneshya came down the hall. Luke looked disgruntled, but Aneshya was all smiles. Just like always.

"I got my book report done." She beamed. "I bet I get an A."

"I'm sure you will, sweetie."

"She always gets an A." Luke said, ruffling his sister's hair as he passed. Aneshya squawked at him and smoothed her hair but grinned, soaking up the praise.

There was a knock at the door. I glanced out the front window as I made my way to the door, surprised to see Knox. He'd been here almost every day since we'd moved in but kept his distance from me for the most part, though I'd seen him speaking with Luke and Aneshya once or twice. Which was understandable. He had a niece and nephew he'd never met. I was sure he'd want to get to know them.

"Knox." I smiled as I stepped back, inviting him inside. "It's good to see you." I blinked, my smile faltering. I was an idiot. "I mean, you know, up close and personal. You're usually off by yourself." Would he think I wasn't grateful he watched over us? Because I knew without a doubt Knox was doing exactly that.

He gave me an amused smirk. "Good to see you too, Evelyn. Glad to see you're getting settled."

"You've been here a lot since we moved in. We've settled in because you and Grover have basically seen to our every need." It was a gentle reprimand, but I doubt he caught it. If he did, he didn't pay attention.

"Good. That's what I was aimin' for."

"Hey, Knox." Luke lifted his chin in greeting as he helped Aneshya put on her backpack.

"Luke. Thought I'd give you guys a lift to school." He shrugged. "If you want."

"On your bike?" Luke's eyes got wide, then he looked puzzled. "But how can we all three ride?"

Knox chuckled. "Right. That's not happenin', and I think you know it, you little punk."

Luke grinned, his cover blown. "Never hurts to try, big guy."

"You don't have to do that." It was automatic on my part. I always said that whenever Knox dropped by and offered to take the kids to school. I didn't want him to feel like he was obligated. Besides, I was growing attached to the big man. He looked so much like Danny it was off-putting at first, but he was nothing like his brother.

"Fully aware I don't. Also, I think you know me well enough by now to know I don't do anything I don't want to do."

"If you're sure."

He gave me a cocky grin, like he'd won this round when I had no idea we were even competing. "I'm sure. Mind if I drop in after I get them off to school?"

"I, uh… W-what?" My heart pounded. Knox. In my home. With me. Alone. Grover had gone to run some errands he said would take all day and to not expect him before the kids got home from school. It was both a fantasy and utterly terrifying. Because, like it or not, smart or not, I was becoming attached to Knox. And we'd barely said two words to each other.

"It wasn't a hard question, Evelyn. Either you're good with me coming back to talk with you or you're not."

"This is more your home than it is mine. You don't need permission to come over." It was a non-answer, and we both knew it.

"It's fine." Luke said, looking from one of us to the other. "Come over anytime you want." He grinned. "Especially if no one else is here but my mom."

If he'd been closer, I'd have head slapped him. My darling son just grinned and urged his sister out the door.

"You're in big trouble when you get home." I pointed a finger at him and tried to look stern.

"No, I'm not." He waved cheerfully.

Knox grinned like an ape. "See you in half an hour."

"You want some breakfast?" If he was coming over, I might as well feed him.

The smile Knox gave me was positively wicked. "Absolutely."

I gasped, feeling the blood rush to my face. How the hell could he make that exchange sound… sexual? He winked at me before ushering the kids out the door. Luke glanced at me over his shoulder and grinned.

Well, shit.

As the door shut and I heard Knox and the kids

chatting on their way to his truck, I peeked out the door. It had only been a couple of weeks since one of these brothers had turned my world upside down. Was I a fool for letting Knox get close? I still didn't know where he'd been this whole time, and it wasn't my business. But what if he disappeared again? Grover had told me he'd thought Knox was dead all this time.

I hadn't been close to Danny. If it hadn't been for Luke and Aneshya, I'd have left him years ago. But we weren't married, and since he'd never threatened or abused any of us in any way, I'd never keep his children from him if they wanted to see him. I hadn't spent much time one-on-one with Knox, but he'd quietly but persistently inserted himself into my life. Even though we weren't romantically involved with each other, if something happened to Knox, I wasn't sure I could ever let go. Especially knowing he'd come back from the dead once already.

Breakfast consisted of biscuits and gravy, eggs, hash browns, and sausage. Thankfully, there had been leftovers of everything other than the eggs, which were easy to make. I'd just taken them off the stove when there was another knock at my door.

My heart leapt. God! I felt like a stupid schoolgirl with her first crush. It was insane.

"It's not been thirty minutes, but I just finished the eggs. I take it traffic was better than usual?" I stopped dead in my tracks. "Danny."

"Hey, honey." He smiled at me. Like nothing had happened. Like he hadn't been gone for more than two weeks. Like the last time I saw him hadn't been in the hospital where he was sitting with his pregnant wife who was also the owner of our building.

Like he hadn't abandoned his children. I could understand him going after his pregnant wife -- or any pregnant woman -- in a burning building. She'd been just as capable as me, but she was in advanced pregnancy. I wasn't. But him not even calling to check on us, on his kids, that I couldn't forgive.

"You shouldn't be here, Danny."

"Why not? This is my home more than it is yours." He stuck his chin up. I wasn't used to him being belligerent after he knew he was in trouble. He always backed down, admitted how wrong he was, what a piece of shit he was, and that he didn't deserve the wonderful family he'd been given. Now, he had the intention of trying to get me to take him back. I'd seen him act this way with people in his life, usually his father. It didn't matter to him if I wanted him back or not. He simply didn't care.

"It's your father's house. You shouldn't enter unless invited inside."

"He's *my* dad. I don't have to ask permission." Yeah. This was a side of Danny I'd seen before, but never directed at me. He was cutting me out of his life. Or trying to make me beg him to come back. "Where're the kids?"

"Seriously?" What kind of question was that? It was a school day. They're in school. Duh!

"Yeah, seriously. I wanna see my kids!"

"Well, they're in school. They'll be home about three-fifteen. You're more than welcome to come back then. Whether or not you can stay or even come inside is up to your father."

"I'm not leaving, Evie. I'll wait for them here. Or maybe I'll just go get them myself."

"What's wrong with you?" I yelled at him. This was completely out of character for Danny. Yeah, if he didn't have a use for a person he could be -- and often was -- cutting. But something was very different. He almost seemed... desperate? "We've been here more than two weeks, Danny. You've not called, come by, or tried to get in contact with us in any way. Now you think you get to take my children?"

"Did you try to find me? I coulda been hurt."

"You were in the hospital with your w-wife." I was proud I only stumbled slightly over the word. "Why would you even consider I'd try to find you?"

"If you loved me the way you always said, you would have."

"Look, I don't know what the problem is, but you need to leave."

"Or what? You're in my house. If anyone's leaving, it's you, Evie. All I have to do is call 911. Then you get charged with trespassing and breaking and entering and whatever else they can come up with. Which would go a long way toward me getting custody of Luke and Aneshya."

I gasped. The blood drained from my face. I felt it go and knew I was going to faint.

"I sincerely hope this is your idea of a bad joke, Danny." That voice... I sagged in relief. How could two brothers who look so much alike sound so completely different? And how had I stood Danny's whiny voice all these years? So much time. Wasted. Instead of trying my hardest to make Danny love me. I should have been finding someone who actually would.

Danny whipped around to face Knox. "What are you doing here?"

Knox shrugged. "Like you said. This is my house."

"Dad told me he'd sold the place. Years ago."

"Yes. He did." Knox didn't expound.

"Well, obviously either he lied or you bought it."

"That's none of your business. Neither is Evelyn. Or the kids." Knox didn't sound angry... exactly... More like he was stating a fact. The look in his eyes, though. That told another story. Unless I completely misjudged Knox, right now, he was completely *furious*. I actually backed up a step away from him.

"Luke and Aneshya are my children, Knox. My name's on their birth certificates."

"That's something we'll be discussing later. Right now, though, I think you'd better leave."

"This is between me and Evie. It has nothing to do with you or Pop."

"If it involves Evelyn, it involves Dad and me. We've been the ones who've been on her and the kids' side after they lost everything in that fire. You should have come to at least check on your children. To make sure they weren't hurt in the fire."

"I saw them at the hospital. They were fine."

"Two and a half weeks, Danny," Knox snapped. "Two and a half Goddamned weeks. Not one word from you. Not to Dad. Not to Evelyn. Now you're threatening to take her children and throw her out of the house."

"What is she to you, Knox?"

"I can't answer that question, Danny. Not yet. Like the woman said, come back this afternoon. After three-fifteen."

My knees did give way then, and I collapsed onto the sofa. Knox winked at me.

"What the fuck, Knox? She's *my girlfriend*!"

Knox threw his head back and laughed. Actually guffawed. "Are you shittin' me? You honestly think that after finding you with your pregnant wife, Evelyn is still your girlfriend? Is that truly how you thought this was going to work?"

"I could give two shits, Knox. The only thing I care about is my kids. I want custody of them."

Knox took a threatening step toward his brother. "Over my dead body."

Danny looked from Knox to me. "I'll be back."

"At your own peril, Danny. You hurt anyone in this house, and it will be the last thing you ever do."

With one last venomous look at me, Danny stomped out the door. Knox followed him, then shut and locked the door before turning back to me.

"I'm not going to let anything happen to your kids, Evelyn. No one is going to take them from you. I swear it."

"I can't imagine what's going on with him." I shook my head, my voice soft. I wanted to avoid the conversation to come as long as I could. What did he mean when he said he didn't know what I was to him yet? Was he merely trying to keep his brother off-balance? Or did he intend to define our relationship and his place in my life as the children's uncle?

"He's never acted like this before?"

"I was just thinking to myself how cold and distant he was. He has no intention of trying to be part of my life. He didn't once act like he regretted anything. And honestly, I feel sorry for his wife. I also feel guilty and like so much of a fool I don't deserve to breathe. I lived with Danny for thirteen years! And he was married the whole time? How did I not know?"

"Didn't look to me like his wife knew anything either. He's good at deception."

"Why in the world would he do this, Knox? He obviously intends to stay with his wife, which I'm oddly grateful for. But, with her so close to having her own baby, I can't imagine she'd want his children by a secret lover living with her."

"That's something I intend to find out. But that can wait. You and I need to talk."

"Is this where you tell me to leave?"

Impatience flashed over Knox's face. "I thought we were past this. I promised you no one would take away your children, Evelyn."

"Then what is it?"

Knox took a slow step toward me, a wicked smile on his face. It was the smile of an alpha. A predator. "Until I walked in here and saw Danny with you, I wasn't sure exactly what I was going to say to you."

"You're going to have to explain, Knox. I don't understand."

"I'd planned to tell you I wanted to be part of Luke and Aneshya's lives. That I wanted us to have a good relationship. But as a brother and sister-in-law. I didn't know how awkward it would be for you, and wanted to establish some boundaries."

"Don't remind me," I muttered.

He chuckled. "Yeah, well, I decided I don't care how awkward it is because you might not be mine yet, but you're not Danny's anymore, either. And I intend to make you mine."

Chapter Six

Knox

What came out of my mouth wasn't what I'd intended to say. True, I'd decided to take my dad's advice and feel Evelyn out -- no pun intended -- but when I saw Danny standing there, something akin to panic seized me. That feeling quickly turned to an ice-cold anger when I actually heard the topic of conversation. The second I uttered the words, however, I knew they were true. Evelyn was going to be mine. I'd show her how a woman should be treated, and I'd show her kids what a dad was really like.

"What?"

"Oh, I think you heard me, Evelyn." She backed up a step. So I moved forward a step.

"I can't be in that kind of relationship with you." Shaking her head, Evelyn continued to back up until she was against the wall. She jumped when her back met the drywall. I knew I had to tread carefully here. I was on the hunt and Evelyn was my prey.

"Sure, you can. I've seen you watching me. Unless I'm mistaken, you like what you see."

"Are you suggesting I jump from one brother to another? Your father would be mortified. He's been so good to me, Knox…" She shook her head, her eyes wide. "I don't want him thinking badly of me."

I grinned. "Sweetheart, who do you think kicked my ass to come talk to you? My father thinks you should have been with me to begin with." Reaching out to her, I stroked her cheek lightly with my fingers. "Regardless, if you don't want me, if you aren't ready to move on yet, I fully intend to take care of you and Luke and Aneshya. I have some things to work out with… well, Lemon and her man."

"His name is Rocket. Like yours is Knox."

"That's right. Lemon tell you?"

"Yes. She said you're part of a motorcycle club called Grim Road. I'm also not supposed to say anything outside your group."

"Lemon told you about Grim Road?" Interesting.

"Just that everything there is on the down low." Her breathing quickened, and I saw her glance at my lips. Her gaze came back to my eyes but kept straying downward.

"Good. So Lemon has accepted you too."

"The kids…"

"Are gonna be fine. You heard Luke. He's fine with us being together."

"I don't even know if I like you or not."

"You say as you're staring at my mouth. Wanting me to kiss you, baby?"

Her gaze snapped to mine. "I am not staring at your mouth!"

There was no way to prevent my laughter, though it sounded darker and more dangerous than full of humor. Yeah. Now that the idea had set in my mind, there wasn't a chance in hell I wasn't making her mine.

"Yeah, you are, baby." I pressed closer, my body touching hers but not trapping her. If she really wanted to push me away, I wouldn't fight her. But I didn't think she wanted me to go. "My dad's right. You're as interested in me as I am you."

"No, I'm not." She shook her head slightly, but her voice was barely above a whisper.

"Oh, I think you are." I grinned at her, leaning in slowly as I did. "Tell you what. I'm going to kiss you. We'll test exactly how much you're not interested. How does that sound?"

"I --" She gulped, but she lowered her eyes again, looking at my mouth.

"That's what I thought."

I closed the gap between us, brushing my lips over hers in a gentle caress.

Her lips were soft and sweet, just as I knew they would be. After a brief moment of hesitation, her body relaxed. A shuddering sigh escaped her as she twined her arms around my neck.

My dick was rock-hard now. I wanted nothing more than to take her right then, but that was most definitely not on my agenda today. This was about gentling her. Letting her learn my touch. One thing I'd known but had yet to experience was exactly how special this woman really was. The way she melted against me, moaning softly into my mouth as she trembled, gave me a preview of just how passionate a lover she would be. That she was letting me see a glimpse of this side of her told me she was comfortable around me. Still, I wouldn't push her too far. Not yet. But I would push a little further.

She tasted like strawberries and the sweetest sin, her body pressing against mine as though she couldn't help herself. My tongue flicked out to trace her lower lip and she gasped, only inviting me in more.

I took her mouth, sealing my lips to hers, drinking her cries as she offered them to me. Her tongue dueled with mine, exploring, learning me and how I moved when I kissed her. I brought my hands up, cupping her face, as if to memorize her, memorize this moment. This was our first kiss, and I never wanted to forget it.

"Wow…" Evelyn brought trembling fingers to her lips. "That was…"

"Yeah, baby. It was."

"Will you…" She cleared her throat, swallowing. "Will you do it again?"

I grinned. "Do what again?"

Her lips twitched upward, even though I could tell she was still shell-shocked. "Kiss me."

I raised an eyebrow. "You want me to kiss you? Again?" When she nodded, I grinned. "Oh, no, Evelyn. You were hesitant before. I need to be absolutely sure this is what you want." I kissed the side of her neck because I couldn't help myself. "So I need you to tell me again." Another kiss to her neck. "What do you want?"

"Oh my." She moaned. "Kiss me again, please."

I chuckled against her skin, knowing she was as weak for my touch as I was for hers. "As you wish." Then I kissed her again, capturing her lips with mine. This time, I poured some of my hunger into my kiss, needing her to know exactly what I wanted from her. It went beyond the sexual, though there was plenty of sexual hunger. I wanted this woman for my own. Just like I told her I did.

As we kissed, her body molded against mine, her soft curves pressed yearningly against my hardness. There was no denying the attraction now, and it filled me with a heady sense of victory even though I'd never wanted a woman of my own. Not like I wanted Evelyn.

My hands traveled down her back, beneath her shirt, to the curve of her hips, gripping her as my mouth devoured hers. Her hands roamed too, exploring my muscles, running up and down my back. She was giving as good as she got, and damn if it didn't turn me on that much more.

"That's it, baby." When I spoke next to her ear, she whimpered, turning her head to chase my mouth with hers. "You want more?"

"Yes," she whispered. "More. Please, Knox."

Her hands, those elegant, clever hands slid to my shoulders, digging her nails in as if she were using me as an anchor. I didn't mind; it just spurred me on. I kissed her again, this time rougher, tasting every inch of her luscious mouth.

My tongue invaded her mouth with an intensity I'd never delivered to a woman before. The harder I kissed Evelyn, the more I could taste desire on her lips, and she leaned into me, her arms tightening around my neck.

She clung to me so sweetly, her scent wrapping around me like a cloak. Fresh, ocean air and lavender tickled my nose, making me inhale deeply just to take in her sweet fragrance.

I tried to pull back from her but Evelyn clung to me, holding me to her tightly. She met my kiss with her own, darting her own tongue tentatively against mine. The second she did, something inside me settled. Evelyn wanted this. She might not be ready for me to make her mine completely, but she liked the way I made her body feel.

I nipped at her lower lip gently, and she moaned softly. I groaned at the sound and deepened the kiss even more, my tongue swirling around hers playfully. When I pulled away slightly, she whimpered in protest, wanting more. I chuckled against her lips before capturing them again.

I slid my hand downward along her back, tracing the curve of her waist and hips possessively before cupping one hip firmly through the thin material of her long shirt and yoga pants.

Evelyn gasped, looking up into my eyes with such need and lust it made my dick throb. I ached with the need to fuck her.

"God, what you do to me, woman!" My growl was rough, almost angry sounding.

"You're doing the same thing to me." Her voice was husky but soft. She sounded like a woman who'd been screaming all night in pleasure. That was something I was determined to make happen, no matter how long it took to get her there.

I pulled back, framing her beautiful face with my hands. Her long, dark hair was a halo of curls around her face, caressing my hands as I stroked her cheek. "How far do you want this to go, Evelyn? Because I want you. Want to fuck you all fuckin' day, take you back to Grim Road, and fuck you some more until you know without a doubt that you're mine."

"Knox." Her little gasp sent shivers through me. "I don't... I don't know."

I shook my head slowly. "Oh, I think you do. But I get it. You're not ready." I gave her a self-deprecating smile. "If I'm honest with you and myself, I'm not sure I'm ready for all that means either. I only admitted it to myself when I saw Danny here with you."

I let my forehead fall against hers and took several deep breaths. She tilted her head up and kissed my bottom lip before rubbing her face against my bearded cheek.

"I don't think I've ever wanted to have sex more than I do right now in this moment." She made the confession softly but looking up at me so I could see the truth of it in her eyes. "But I don't want you to think badly of me. I don't... that is, I've only ever had one lover and I stayed with him for thirteen years."

"And you're afraid to give yourself to another man so soon?"

"Yes." Then she shook her head, lowering her gaze. "No. I mean. Not exactly." She looked back up at me. "You feel different than Danny ever did." Her brows furrowed. "What I mean is, I never really felt like I'd found my place with Danny. I think I always knew there was something wrong. At first, I think I did what he wanted because I didn't know I could or even should leave him after our first couple of times. I thought I should stay with him until I knew for sure I didn't want to be with him. But as time went on…"

"You fell into a pattern. A habit."

"Yeah. I guess I did."

"And now? How does it feel with me?"

Tears filled Evelyn's eyes, but she smiled up at me. "Like this is where I'm supposed to be."

Chapter Seven

Evelyn

If someone had told me a month ago I'd be in the arms of Danny's long-dead brother, I'd have laughed until I peed myself. The idea was absurd on multiple levels. Before.

Before I found out I'd been the other woman for our entire thirteen years together. Before Danny left not only me but our children without a backward glance. Before he turned up at the house his father told him he'd sold, the house where our children and I now lived with his father, and threatened to take the children who'd become my whole life.

Before... I realized how much he didn't love me.

Before I realized how much I didn't love him.

Now I stood here, in the arms of a man I'd first thought looked exactly like Danny, only older. Harder. Battle-hardened. The thing was, over the last two and a half weeks, I'd learned the difference between Danny and Knox. Knox had no reason to care for me, to care for my children. He simply did what had to be done. He made sure we had everything we needed, including his time.

Knox had been with us every day when I got the kids off to school. He'd been here every evening when they got home. I'd seen him during the day close to the house. Sometimes he worked in the yard. Sometimes, he repaired something on the house outside. When his dad was here, he'd work on things inside. He was always kind and respectful. In fact, this was the first time he'd indicated in any way that he wanted anything from me. Oh, we'd spoken. Talked over breakfast or coffee during a break -- I worked from home, and he often took his breaks with me. Even made sure I stopped for ten or fifteen minutes when I'd been at it too long. Knox was fast becoming my rock. And I'd be lying to myself if I said that didn't scare me.

"I never cared for Danny. Not really. I mean, he's the father of my children, and I love them more than life itself, but he's never been around. Not like I needed him to be." Did I imagine Knox stiffened? No. With his body so close to mine, I could feel something was wrong. "Did I say something wrong?"

"What?" He looked confused before his eyes widened. "NO! You said nothing wrong, honey. Nothing at all." He sighed, shaking his head slightly. "I was just thinking about something I told my father when he told me about your relationship with my brother and how Danny was never around."

"He wasn't. Not much. I'm beginning to question whether he ever had a job at all. Lord knows I never saw money from it. He didn't help with anything."

"This may be the one thing that changes your mind to give me a chance."

"I don't understand."

"Did Lemon tell you anything about what we do in Grim Road?"

"A little. She said sometimes the members have to go on missions away from here. Like a paramilitary group."

"Yeah. It's a little more complicated than that, but at one point in time all of us have been in the military. Now that Lemon set her foot down, Rocket and Bear go through each mission sent to Crush. He and his brother, Byte, are our intel officers. They make sure that any mission we take is not only worthy of us risking our lives, but achievable with a reasonable amount of risk."

"So they've made it as safe as they can."

That surprised me. That Evelyn would see it that way. "Yes. But there are times when I'll have to be away. I told my father I was afraid you'd be trading one absent man for another."

"How did he respond?"

I snorted a laugh. "He told me to quit. That a man takes care of his family. As much as I'd love to do just that, I'm part of Grim Road. If they need me, I have to answer the call." I tightened my arms around her. "But what I can do is make sure there is always someone protecting you and the kids. If you choose to live here, I'll make sure there is someone from my club here with you at all times. If you'd rather come to our compound to live with me, I'll take all of you -- Dad included -- away from here. At the compound, you'd have the whole club to protect you."

"This isn't something I can give you an answer about now, Knox. For one thing, I haven't talked to Luke and Aneshya about it. Obviously, Luke wants us together, if what he said earlier was any indication, but there's a lot to consider."

"You should consider everything. I'd never push you into something like this without letting you think it through."

I took a deep breath. The wild, musky scent of him mingled with leather and gasoline like an unorthodox aphrodisiac. "I don't know what the future holds or what I should do to take care of my children, but I want this moment with you, Knox. If it's all I ever get, I want to experience it all. Just once."

"Oh, you'll get it more than once, honey." He smirked as he lifted me into his arms and carried me down the hall to my bedroom. "Ain't just talkin' 'bout today either. I will do whatever it takes to convince you to give me a shot." He entered my room and kicked the door shut. "Whatever I have to do to earn that chance, I'll do. No matter what." Then he scowled. "Especially if it has something to do with kicking my brother's ass."

That got a surprised giggle out of me. Knox stopped and gave me a stern look. "You think I'm playing, but I'm fuckin' serious. I intend to make my brother pay for what happened here today, to say nothing of everything else. Threatening to take your kids is a step too far. Especially when he's the one in the wrong."

"I don't want to think about him right now, Knox. I want you to kiss me again. This time, I don't want you to stop until we're both so exhausted we can't do it anymore."

"Who am I to argue with that?"

He laid me down on the bed, covering me with his large frame as he found my lips with his again. I reveled at being pinned beneath him, loving his weight pressing me into the mattress. Every movement of his body against mine seemed to be designed to drive me insane. It felt like every nerve ending I had was on fire, but in the most delicious way.

Knox trailed his kisses down my neck, flicking his tongue against the sensitive spot where my collarbone met my shoulder. I moaned into his mouth.

"God, Knox. I never expected this. I never expected anything to feel this good." My words were a mere whisper, but he grunted, understanding me. Probably in more ways than I was prepared for. I hadn't known Knox long, but his father had fed me a steady stream of accolades and stories. Looking back, perhaps he'd been trying to get me to be more comfortable around Knox. So I'd let Knox have a chance with me? That seemed a little far-fetched, but I had to wonder. Especially with Knox saying his father had pushed him into getting to know me.

"Can't say I expected it either, honey." He kissed me again before trailing his lips down my jaw line to my neck. I arched my back as he reached the top of my shirt with his lips. His hands slipped under my shirt, rubbing my skin from the waist of my pants up the sides of my chest.

He pushed my shirt over my breasts and tugged it off, leaving me there in my bra. Knox kissed the swell of one breast while unfastening the bra clasp with his other hand.

His lips were devilishly soft, sending tingles down my spine. I couldn't stop the moan that escaped my lips as he suckled the peak of one breast, then the other. The sensation was almost too much to bear. My hands wound their way into his hair, holding him to me. I wished I'd worn something sexier, but this was so far from the way I thought this day would go it wasn't even funny.

"You're so beautiful, Evie. Every inch of you."

He reached back between his shoulder blades and pulled his shirt over his head. The magnificence of tattooed skin and hard muscle he revealed was like something out of my most fevered fantasies. I ran my hands across his chest, the slight dusting of hair abrading my palms.

"You're beautiful too." I don't know why I said that. A man like Knox probably wouldn't appreciate it, but he was. He was cut like a Greek statue. A god with the power to consume a mortal woman like me. Still, I craved more of his touch.

The corners of his lips lifted, and he shook his head. "Guys ain't beautiful."

"You are." I let my hands feather over his broad

shoulders and muscled triceps. "Never seen a man so perfectly made." My voice was a husky whisper. I sounded as in awe of him as I felt.

Knox slid his hand to my waistband, sliding my pants and panties over my hips and down my legs before tossing them onto the floor. I trembled as he lay back on top of me.

"This goes as far as you want it, honey. If you want me to make you come over and over until you pass out, I'll do that. But I don't have to fuck you. Not if you don't want me to."

"Don't even think about backing out now," I snapped. "You started it, you have to finish."

That got a bark of laughter from Knox. "God, this is going to be one hell of an adventure." He kissed me again before sliding down my body, kissing his way to the top of my mound.

My body arched as his mouth teased my pussy just above my clit, and I moaned in pleasure. Our connection had grown rapidly despite having only known each other for a short time. Which should have scared me. After all, I'd just ended a thirteen-year relationship with this man's brother.

"Can't say I expected this. But I'll be Goddamned if I'm giving you up just because I wasn't prepared for you."

His words inflamed me further, and I canted my hips up to meet his mouth. "Knox," I cried out his name as he slid two long fingers inside of me, curling them just right, and I nearly went off the edge.

"That's it, baby. So fuckin' wet."

He licked me from top to bottom, his tongue swirling around my clit before he sucked it gently into his mouth. My back bowed off the bed, my hands fisting in the sheets with a strangled cry. He was right,

I thought as wave after wave of pleasure crashed over me in a wild crescendo. I knew I was wet, could feel moisture on my inner thighs. Hell, I could feel the gush of moisture as that orgasm exploded within me.

"So fuckin' beautiful." Knox's words were said almost reverently. When I looked down at him between my thighs, his gaze was focused squarely on mine.

Very slowly, he moved to his knees, retaining a hold on my thighs and draping them over his as he settled closer to my apex.

"This first time might go quicker than I'd like, but unless you stop me, I'm getting ready to fuck you good, Evelyn." He pulled out his wallet from his back pocket and opened it. I stiffened, thinking he was going to insult me in the worst possible way. If he threw down some bills, making this a transaction... Yeah. Not only would I shatter, but I'd probably kill him. Then my kids would be left with Danny as a father. The thought was sickening.

"Don't look at me like that," Knox snapped. "I'm not above paying a woman for sex but not you. Never you." He plucked two condoms from his wallet and tossed them on the bed beside me.

"I'm sorry." My arms went reflexively over my breasts to cover myself. "Sorry."

Immediately, his expression softened. "My brother really did a number on your self-esteem, didn't he?"

Had he? I hadn't really thought about it until this moment. "I'm so sorry, Knox. I didn't mean --"

"Shh... It's all right. You didn't do anything wrong. I shouldn't have snapped at you, and I should have explained."

"It's a fucking condom, Knox." I sniffled. "Where

else are you gonna keep it? Pretty sure most men carry one in their wallet."

Instead of blowing me off or laughing at me, Knox stretched back down on top of me. "Given that you've spent more than a decade with a man who disrespected you in every way he could, that he fathered two children with you but was never committed to the relationship, you have every right to question my sincerity, Evelyn."

"You're not your brother."

"No. I'm not. I think you know that, too." He shifted so he could rest his hand on my chest. "But your heart needs protecting. It's not going to accept anyone so quickly, no matter what your mind tells it."

"I'm not sure you're right about that. It was more my pride. Because the second I saw Danny in this house, and the second I saw you come in after him, I knew I'd never felt anything for Danny. Even the affection I'd had for him when we first got together faded a long time ago. He was a shadow in our lives. A ghost. Nothing more."

He tilted his head at me, his brows narrowing together. "You didn't love him." It wasn't a question.

"No. And I know that for certain because I was never drawn to him the way I'm drawn to you."

That must have been the exact right thing to say because Knox gave me the sexiest grin I'd ever seen on a man. "Oh, baby. You made a mistake there."

I blinked, confused. "Huh?"

"You admitted how much you want me. I think you meant you want me more than just in your bed, too. I think you want me in your life."

I shook my head, then stopped, really thinking about that. "You're already in my life. Have been, since the fire. It's been you and your father. True, we've not interacted that much, but did we really need to? My kids love you. All I hear is 'Uncle Knox.'"

His grin widened. "Good." Then his expression grew serious. "I never even tried to stay away from you, Evelyn. I didn't want to get involved, but the second I saw you in that burning building, making sure your children got to safety even as you were trying to look for that fucking prick Danny, I knew I couldn't." He kissed me again, tenderly, taking his time before he continued to speak. "So, I'm gonna stay right here. Ain't goin' nowhere. And I ain't never, ever, going to disrespect you the way Danny did."

I knew I probably looked like a deer in the headlights. The man was intense and possessive, and I was loving every fucking second of it. "OK." It was all I could manage. If I tried to talk through my feelings right now, I'd cry. If I cried, he'd likely stop. There was no way I was going to miss out on the opportunity to be with this man. "I'll take this one day at a time, Knox. Just promise me you'll give everything to me straight. I can handle honest rejection." I sighed. "All right, it would still hurt something fierce. But I can take it better than you just up and disappearing, or me seeing you with your pregnant wife after worrying myself to death you were still in a burning building looking for me and the kids."

"That, baby, is something you'll never have to worry about. I don't cheat. Ever. That came from my dad. He always told us growing up that a real man protects his family. No matter the cost. That's what I intend to do."

Before I could say anything else, Knox kissed me again, taking his time and making me relax back into the moment. "So delicious," he murmured. "Like a drug I'm rapidly becoming addicted to."

He pushed himself back up to sit between my legs, then unfastened his jeans and slid them down his thighs. His cock bobbed proudly, the head glistening with a drop of precum.

"Oh…" I reached out automatically, wanting to touch him. Then I froze. I'd only had sex with one man in my life. Danny had been my first and only lover. Were men OK with a woman touching without permission?

"Touch it, baby." His whisper was the devil in my ear. So fucking wicked and naughty. I was helpless not to reach out again to run my hand up and down his thick, hard dick. He groaned, his head falling back. "That's it. God, that feels good!"

His words gave me confidence I hadn't realized I needed. Had I ever been able to satisfy Danny in bed? Lord knew he'd never made me feel even a quarter of what Knox already had. For the first time since the very first time, sex was an adventure. And I knew it had everything to do with the man himself and not simply a new lover.

Knox reached over to snag one of the condoms he'd tossed to the side of the bed. Tearing open the package, he gave me a wicked smile before rolling it over his cock.

"Now," he said, slowly lowering himself to cover me again. "I'm gonna fuck you. Gonna make you sweat. Scream my name. When this is finally over, you're gonna know you belong to me. And I belong to you."

With a slowness I realized I didn't want, Knox entered me in a smooth, wet glide. I gasped, arching up to meet his thrust.

"Mmm… Someone likes that."

"Yes. More." My breathy sigh was embarrassing.

I wasn't a virgin. Not in any sense of the word. But I'd never felt anything to compare to this. My body was on fire! Every single nerve ending I had was a mass of sensation. When he moved inside me, it put the perfect amount of friction on my clit as well as hit that spot inside me that drove me crazy.

Knox grunted and kissed me again, continuing to move. He wrapped his strong arms around me, settling me right where he wanted before speeding up his movements slightly. It was a perfect blend of restraint and eagerness. He shuddered above me, and his body broke out into a sweat. Same as mine. Wicked flicks of his tongue against mine made the whole thing that much more intense. The man knew how to pleasure a woman, that was for sure. And I didn't care about how many other lovers he'd had. He was with me now. Maybe for a short time. Maybe longer. But in this moment, right now, he was mine.

When my whimpers and moans increased in volume and frequency, Knox moved faster. I slid my hands down his back to grip his ass, trying to urge him to move faster. The big oaf simply chuckled and kept the same slow, steady pace.

"Don't be impatient. We've got alllll day." He sounded lazy and contented as he trailed kisses to my neck before latching on, sucking on the tender skin.

I screamed as the extra stimulation was exactly what I needed to push me over the edge. His name on my lips was like a prayer. A strangled plea for deliverance. My pussy contracted, and I could feel his cock swell inside me.

"Oh, God! Knox!"

"That's it, baby." His breathing was ragged, and he sped up slightly only to shudder and slow back to his original pace. "Can feel you squeezin' my cock.

Tryin' to take my cum."

"Yes! Oh, please! Please!"

"You want my cum? Want it deep inside you, baby girl?"

"YES!" That last scream was the evidence of my undoing. Another, stronger, orgasm tore through me with a violent intensity I'd never experienced. I screamed and screamed.

And screamed.

Knox either took that as a sign to give me what I asked for or he'd reached the end of his endurance. Either way, he pounded into me, giving me a tooth-clattering ride. Then, with his own hoarse shout, he buried himself as deep inside me as he could. His cock pulsed with every spurt of cum filling the condom.

For long moments, we both lay there, just trying to breathe. For some reason, I started to giggle. Then Knox chuckled. Then we both laughed, clinging to each other where we lay with Knox still buried inside me.

"Sweet, God," he breathed, stroking a damp lock of hair off my forehead. "You're so fuckin' beautiful."

"That was amazing."

"It was. And if you give me a bit to recover, we'll do it again." He grinned at me and leaned in to kiss me once more. "We've got all fuckin' day."

I sighed, stretching and rubbing against Knox like a contented kitten. Hell, I felt like a contented kitten. "That sounds like the best idea ever."

Chapter Eight

Knox

Danny didn't show up that afternoon. In fact, he didn't show up the following day or even the following week. It had been a month since I'd seen or heard from him. Even Crush had been unable to find much. From the looks of things, Danny and his wife had split, but he was still trying to get back into her good graces. He'd already tried to empty their checking account, but she'd moved everything to a new bank in only her name. I told my dad about what had happened the second he stepped on the place, though.

"If he shows up here, your mother may turn over in her grave, but I swear, I'll kill him myself." I wasn't sure I'd ever seen my dad this angry. "He's not been a father to those children since they were born. How dare he try to start now?"

"I can't imagine his wife wants the children of his mistress. There has to be more going on."

My father looked at me. "Find out what he's up to, Knox."

"Already on it, Pop. Should hear back from my guys soon."

"Good, because I don't plan on losing more of the most important people in my life. Not again." Dad went inside, slamming the door for once.

I cursed low under my breath. I didn't have to ask what he meant. He was talking about me and Mom. He'd said he essentially lost us at the same time. And we both knew if Danny got the kids, he'd use them as leverage. For money. He'd bleed us dry and make the kids' lives miserable. Those two loved Evelyn. Watching them all together, it was easy to see.

And Evelyn loved them just as much.

The next few weeks passed uneventfully. I'd pulled Luke aside and told him to watch out for his sister and not to leave school with anyone he didn't know.

"It's Danny, isn't it." Luke didn't phrase it as a question. The kid knew. "He coming for us?"

"Not sure." I gave him an encouraging smile. "I'd just rather be safe than sorry."

Luke studied me for a few seconds, then seemed to come to a decision. "I saw him." He lifted his chin toward a hole in the fence. That hole had been there since I was a kid. Danny and I had put it there so we could sneak into the neighbor's yard and play in their pool when they were gone. "He tried to get me to come to him, but I got Aneshya and went inside."

Everything inside me stilled. "He what?"

"I'm pretty sure he thought he'd get my attention and that Aneshya would follow me." Luke shook his head. "I don't want nothing to do with him no more."

I had to tread carefully here. Even with what happened, that both Luke and Aneshya knew Danny was married to another woman and that Luke at least knew what that meant, Evelyn had been very careful not to speak badly of Danny around them. She never indicated why, but I was sure she just didn't think it was appropriate to badmouth the kids' father. He'd never hurt any of them physically, hadn't verbally abused them. Sure, he was neglectful and that was its own abuse, but she tried to let them have the information and make their own conclusions.

"That's your decision, Luke. You can talk to your mother about it if you want. But I don't think she's going to make you have a relationship with him if you don't want it."

"He hurt my mom." Luke lifted his chin, angry in the extreme. "He never hit her or anything, but that day in the hospital, I could see it on Mom's face."

"Yeah, buddy. He did."

"I don't want nothin' to do with anyone who hurts my mom." That was said with the twelve-year-old looking straight into my eyes. I got the message.

"I understand. Completely."

That seemed to be what Luke needed. He stuck out his hand and I took it immediately. "I'm Mom's protector now. I ain't big or strong enough to do much yet, but you are. So as her protector, I'm putting you in charge of keeping her safe. And keeping Danny away from her."

I straightened, my grip on Luke's hand tightening fractionally. "On my honor, Luke. I'll keep her safe. In all respects."

He nodded, then I let his hand go and he turned, heading back inside the house as I scrubbed a hand over my face. I hoped and prayed Dad saw Danny first. If it was me, there was the possibility no one would see the swine ever again.

Luke looked out over the big backyard. "You know, this place is pretty big."

"Yeah. It is. Dad always hated mowing it, but my mom wanted a big yard. She used to have flower beds everywhere." I smiled at the memory.

"Mom always said she wanted a house with a really big place to put a garden. She said her parents used to grow their own fruits and vegetables. She said she misses stuff like that."

I stroked my beard thoughtfully. "You think she'd like something like that here?"

With a shrug, Luke looked up at me. "Dunno. Just sayin'."

Oh… challenge given.

"I see. Well. I might have to talk to Dad. See what he thinks."

"It's his place."

"Yep. But I'm bettin' he'd enjoy seeing your mom happy."

"What about you?"

I took my time, really thinking about my answer to that question. "I think your mom deserves to be happy more than just about anyone I know. And I'd love to see the smile on her face."

That must have been the exact right thing to say because Luke actually grinned. "You might be all right, Knox."

I was about to follow Luke inside when Evelyn pulled into the driveway. Likely with a trunk full of groceries. Immediately, four guys approached us from where they'd been sitting on their bikes just off the property and out of sight. Lemon had ordered a protection detail for Evelyn, the kids, and my dad. They generally stayed out of the way, but when Evelyn came home with groceries, they all came out of hiding to infiltrate our happy home. I couldn't help but smile. Evelyn loved to cook for us all, and the guys appreciated it.

"Hey, Evie!" Wolf, a guy who was normally very secretive and withdrawn, smiled as he approached Evelyn. "Whatcha got there? Need help carrying it in?"

Evelyn graced him with a beautiful smile, and an ugly green-eyed monster reared its ugly head inside me. "Mine," I growled. Evelyn just laughed, stepping into me and lacing her arms around my neck. She went up on her tiptoes and kissed me gently. Which wouldn't do. So I wrapped my arms around her, bent her backward, and gave her a deep, proper kiss.

Catcalls all around.

"Get a room, you two."

"Someone's staking a claim. You got her property vest yet?"

"Jesus, Knox. Never saw you kiss a woman like that before."

Everyone laughed at me. Which, fuck them anyway.

When I ended the kiss, Evelyn looked adorably embarrassed and dazed. Also like she was more than ready to go find that room.

"Never wanted to kiss a woman like that before. Just makin' sure you dumbasses know Evelyn is mine. Not yours."

"They know." Evelyn snuggled in closer. She'd become more comfortable with our relationship and how she could touch me. She loved snuggling. Adored it. I never had, but with Evelyn, I was becoming addicted. I loved the closeness with her. Being able to pull her into my lap and kiss her or just hold her was a luxury I never knew I needed. And I learned all this about myself in the space of a few weeks. "I need to talk to Lemon about getting some better cooks in your compound because clearly your men don't get enough to eat."

"Oh, they get plenty," I groused. "They're just growing boys."

"Who love your woman's cooking." Wolf grinned at me before snagging a couple of the bags in the trunk to carry inside. On his way, he leaned in and kissed Evelyn's cheek.

"Not cool, man. I will get even."

"Still worth it." He winked at Evelyn and continued on. Evelyn giggled and buried her face in my chest. I chuckled and kissed the top of her head.

She still didn't know everything about us, but I'd tried to feed her small things from time to time.

"I'll give you something to laugh at," I growled at Evelyn before picking her up and throwing her over my shoulder, marching into the house with her as I clamped an arm over her thighs to hold her steady while tickling her with the other hand.

The other guys had snagged grocery bags from the trunk along with Wolf and were carrying them inside. I'd just made it to the steps of the front porch when there was a screeching of tires. Three gunshots rang out in rapid succession, one bullet whizzing past my ear and planting itself into the siding of the house.

Evelyn screamed. I dropped down, covering her with my body even as I scanned the area looking for the shooter.

"Shooter!" I yelled as another shot barely missed us. The bullet ricocheted off the wooden porch and into the glass window of the living room.

I pressed Evelyn down, covering her as completely as I could, my arms wrapped around her head to protect her with my own body.

"Did you see 'em?" Leather and Mace were outside in an instant, standing in front of me and Evelyn, making themselves the target.

"Which way did they go?"

"I heard a vehicle turn the corner," I said, trying to check Evelyn over but still keep an eye on our surroundings. "But I didn't see anyone."

"I'll get Crush on city surveillance. See if he can pull up something in this area and find out who did this." Mace had his phone to his ear. Probably calling Crush or Rocket.

There was a shrill scream from inside the house. I heard someone grunt, then there was a thump.

"Oh, my God!" Evelyn's voice was a strangled croak. "The kids!" She struggled to get up, but I wasn't ready to let her up.

"Calm down, honey. Whoever did this could still be out there."

"Luke! Aneshya!"

"Mom!" That was Aneshya's frightened voice. "Something's wrong with Grandpa!"

"Fuck." I crawled to the door with Evelyn underneath me, moving her along with me until we were inside. Mace and Leather crouched down, keeping a lookout in case whoever had done this wasn't gone. "Dad?"

My father groaned, looking up at me. Blood was pooling on the floor beneath him where he lay on his back.

"Oh no! Grover!" Evelyn was finally able to push out from underneath me and crawled to my dad's side.

There was blood all over his button-up shirt. Evelyn grabbed the collar and yanked, sending buttons flying. His undershirt, too, was soaked in blood. Evelyn shoved it up over his chest to reveal a large exit wound.

Shock and fury washed over me, along with a sense of urgency. I pulled out my phone and called 911. If there was any hope of my dad making it, we had to get him to a hospital immediately.

Evelyn snagged a pillow from the couch and pressed it to his chest with both hands. "Grover, please. Hang on." Her distress was clear. "Luke? Aneshya, where's Luke?"

"I'm here, Mom." The boy was pale and trembling, but he'd brought the first aid kit, obviously trying to help in the only way he knew how. "Do you need this?"

She gave her son a watery smile. "Thank you so much, Luke. That was great thinking, but I think this might be too big for our little kit. Do you think you could take Aneshya to her room and stay with her?"

Luke nodded, never taking his eyes off his grandfather. "I love you, Grandpa," he said, urging Aneshya from the room.

My father tried to speak, but blood bubbled from his lips. He nodded at Luke before turning his gaze to Evelyn. He held her gaze for a long time before raising a bloody hand in my direction.

Immediately, I knelt beside him, grasping his hand firmly in mine. When I did, my father guided my hand to Evelyn's, urging me to take hold. "Keep… her… safe." The sickening gurgle of blood punctuated his words. "Protect…"

"I will, Pop. I'll protect her and the kids. Long as I live. Long as anyone in my club is still alive."

Dad nodded before meeting Evelyn's gaze once more. "Love… him…"

She nodded her head. "I will. I *do*."

My dad smiled. "You're a… good… woman… Evelyn."

"I love you, Grover." Evelyn sobbed out her words. "Please don't… You're like a father to me. I don't want to lose you!"

He smiled. "Daughter… of my… heart. My… son…"

Then my father's eyes went lifeless, his face slackening. The rise and fall of his chest stilled.

Chapter Nine

Evelyn

I was in the bedroom with my children. Aneshya especially was really distraught.

"Will Grandpa be all right, Mommy?"

Luke gave me a look and shook his head. I had no idea what to say because my grief was as sharp as Aneshya's, but I now wasn't the time to let it out. There were too many things I needed to focus on. First was making sure my kids were OK.

"I don't think so, sweetie."

Aneshya dissolved into tears, and I pulled her into my arms. "I'm so sorry, Aneshya."

Luke, bless his heart, wiped his eyes but pulled us both into his embrace. It was obvious he was trying to be what he considered the man. Comforting the women when he was clearly hurting, too. That's how we were when Knox stepped into the room.

His jaw was set, but there were still tears in his eyes he refused to let fall. He took us all three in. Then opened his mouth. Before he could speak, however, Aneshya wiggled out of mine and Luke's embrace and threw herself at him.

"I want my grandpa back, Knox!" She was sobbing as she wrapped her arms and legs around him, crying into his neck.

"I know, honey. I do too." Knox's voice was gruff. He held the child tightly to him, rubbing her back with one hand while the other was clamped around her waist.

I'm not sure who moved first, but the next thing I knew, we were all in Knox's arms. Even Luke sniffled while me and Aneshya cried openly.

We stood like that for several minutes and I was

struck at how it felt like we were a family. This was what Grover wanted. For Knox to be the missing member in our family instead of Danny. I had to admit, Knox felt like more of a mate than Danny ever had.

It struck me then. The entire thirteen-year relationship I had with Danny wasn't really a relationship. Not like I thought it had been. Looking back, the place I'd called home had been a place for Danny to visit a few days at a time before returning to his real home.

I also realized that it wasn't so much the place that was a home, but the people living there. For me that was Luke and Aneshya, Grover, and now Knox. Knox hadn't been living at the house with us, but he was there every single day. Early morning to late into the night. He took care of us. Made sure we had everything we needed. And it wasn't something he asked, either. He was like Grover had been. He saw we needed something he made it happen.

"Knox." A man I hadn't met stood outside the bedroom door with Mace.

"Gonna need a minute, Ringo."

"I know, brother. I'm sorry. But there's someone here you need to see."

"Bleedin' Christ," Knox swore, but he didn't move from our embrace.

"It's important or I wouldn't bother you."

Knox gave us all one last tight squeeze -- the man really was huge -- before leaning down to kiss my lips gently. "I won't be long."

"It's all right, Knox. Take your time."

He gave me a steady look. "I'll be right back."

When I nodded, he followed Ringo out the door.

* * *

Knox

This was all too much. Not only had I lost my father just when I'd come back into his life, but, more importantly, the kids and Evelyn had lost him. I had so much emotion roiling inside me I wasn't sure what to do with it all. Chief among them was rage.

"Who the fuck is it?" I snapped. Ringo was our enforcer. He hadn't come with Wolf, Mace, Leather, and Falcon. Which meant the boys had called in reinforcements when I hadn't thought to do so. Ringo raised an eyebrow at me. I took a deep breath and let it out, trying to calm myself. "Sorry, brother."

"It's all right. I know you've got a lot to process." He moved us farther away from the bedroom before stopping just outside the living room. Where my dad's body still lay. "It's your brother."

My gaze snapped to Ringo's. "What the fuck is he doing here?" I growled, my anger spiking.

Ringo shrugged. "You'll have to ask him that yourself. All we did was prevent him from entering the house, which he's pissed as hell about."

As if on cue, I could hear Danny's raised voice carrying from outside through the house. I couldn't make out his words, but it was obvious he wasn't happy.

"Motherfucker." Not the best idea to take my anger out on my brother, but it was probably going to happen that way.

Ringo grabbed my arm when I started to stomp through the living room to confront my brother. "Wait, Knox. There's something else." I turned to face the enforcer, giving him my full attention. "He was asking about Evelyn. He thought she'd been the one shot."

"She very well could have been." I shuddered to think about that. The rage nearly overwhelmed me. "If

I hadn't been there…"

"You were, Knox." Ringo squeezed my arm again, hard enough to bruise. "You were there, and you protected her, shielded her with your own body. You didn't hesitate. That's what Wolf said. She's your woman and we all know what that means. We also know how that can affect you in this kind of situation. It'd be the same for Rocket or Bullet. Hell, Lemon would go scorched earth if something happened to Rocket, so I get it. But you need to use your head."

"What are you trying to say, Ringo?"

"I got here just a few minutes before Danny did. We haven't called the police or EMS or even the fuckin' coroner. He said he'd heard Evelyn had been killed. Evelyn. By name."

I paused, letting the full meaning of Ringo's words sink in. "No one should have known anything except that maybe they heard gunshots."

Ringo and I locked gazes for several seconds. This… didn't compute. Then it did.

And I. Saw. Red.

Ringo stepped in front of me. "You can't kill him here. And not until we know what's going on. If you can't handle this, I will."

"Like fuck. I'll take care of that fuckin' punk."

"Knox. Not here." Ringo was calm as ever, and it helped to ground me when all I wanted to do was beat the living piss outta my brother.

I took another deep breath, trying to find my calm. Glancing back toward the bedroom where my woman and our kids were, I knew exactly where my calm was.

Our kids.

That thought, more than anything, helped me find something deep inside me I needed to get through this without landing in prison. I not only had my woman to protect, but her children. And yeah, I'd already claimed them as my own. At least, in my heart. This was something I needed to sit down with Luke about and discuss exactly what role he would allow me to play in their lives.

"Good." Ringo nodded and clapped my shoulder. "You found what you needed to do this."

"Yeah." I needed to be as honest with Ringo as I could here. I had the feeling I was going to need every bit of help he and the others could give me. "Not sure how long I can hold it inside, but I've got it."

"Me and the others'll have your back. I'll rein you in if necessary." He tilted his head to the side, warily. "You won't shoot me, will you?"

I barked out a laugh. "If I had a gun, I'd've already shot someone. But I promise I won't fight you too hard."

That seemed to be what Ringo was looking for. Not my promise not to kill him if he tried to pull me out of the situation, but the humor, however dark. I needed it too because I knew now -- I could guarantee -- I wouldn't get myself thrown in prison for killing my brother. Well, ninety percent anyway.

Ringo led the way through the house. In the living room, my gaze was drawn to where my dad had lain lifeless on the floor. They'd moved him and were already cleaning up the blood from the hardwood floor. I raised an eyebrow at Ringo who just nodded at me. I got it. If there was no body, there was nothing to tie me or -- God forbid -- Evie or the kids to Danny's disappearance. 'Cause that fucker was definitely going to disappear.

"You can't keep me from going inside!" Danny hadn't quite committed to getting up in Mace's face, but he was close. "This is my place! And that's my girlfriend who's been shot!"

Mace didn't say anything, just stood in front of Danny with his arms crossed, not letting him onto the porch. Danny caught sight of me and tried to push past Mace, but Wolf and Leather flanked Mace to form an impenetrable wall.

"What the fuck, Denver? Why do you got your goons keeping me out of my own Goddamned house?"

"You good and pissed, Danny?" My voice was a husky growl, which really should have been a clue to the bastard. Then again, Danny had never been the most intelligent. Or, rather, he simply pushed his way through a situation, banking that he could bully or talk his way out of anything negative that arose.

"Goddamned right I'm pissed!" He pointed a finger in my direction. "This house is mine more than it is yours. I don't know why Dad told me he'd sold it when he obviously didn't, but you have no right to keep me out. Especially when my kids are living here. I got every right to see my kids! Now where's Pop? I need to talk to him about making a place for me here so I can be with my family. My kids need me!"

"No, they don't." I shook my head slowly, seeing where he'd go with this. I had every intention of letting him hang himself before dropping this bombshell. Because I had no doubt that, for whatever reason, for whatever goal he intended to accomplish, Danny had been behind this. And Evelyn had been the target.

"What are you talking about? Of course, they do! You think you're gonna take over their care? You disappeared without a trace. We all thought you were dead! You think you can just come in here, show up all happy like you did something grand, and everything goes back to the way it was? News flash, bro. Things don't fuckin' work that way."

"Got nothin' to do with me."

"You might have been hangin' around a few weeks, but we both know you'll take off sooner rather than later. Those kids just lost their mother. They need someone stable in their life. They need me! Their father!"

I took a couple slow steps toward Danny. Off in the distance I heard motorcycles rumbling toward us. I didn't take my eyes from my target, but the others moved to give me room. Which meant the bikes had to be Grim Road MC.

"Evelyn is perfectly fine, and Luke and Aneshya could give two shits if you come home or not."

Danny blinked up at me, shaking his head. "You're lying. They told me -- uh, that is, I heard she'd been shot."

"Well, whoever told you she was shot got it wrong." I tilted my head. "Who was that, anyway? Happened fifteen minutes ago. We haven't called anyone. No one came around the house when shots were fired. No neighbors in this area to come check things out." Narrowing my eyes even more, I took another slow step toward Danny. "How'd you find out?"

I could tell the exact moment when Danny realized he was caught. His eyes widened, and he backed up a step before stopping himself and lifting his chin. "I know what you're implying. If I'd set something like this up, why would I be here now, knowing you would likely be here? And your goons? I'd have driven on when I saw them if I'd had anything to do with this."

"Unless you thought you'd get away with it. Which you might have. If anyone other than the people standing here knew anything about it."

The bikes I'd heard pulled around the corner and parked so that they flanked Danny's car, effectively blocking in the little MINI Cooper. Normally, no one would have used their bikes as a blockade, but the likelihood of a MINI Cooper doing much damage to someone's bike was slim to none.

By the time Danny thought it might be wise to turn tail and run, our company had parked and dismounted their bikes and were approaching. Danny turned but came up short as Rocket, Lemon, Dom, and Apple were moving steadily toward him.

"What's the meaning of this? You touch me and I'll press charges." Danny stuck up a finger, though he pointed at Lemon and Apple. Not Rocket and Dom. No doubt because he felt more comfortable threatening the women than the men as big as my president and sergeant at arms.

"Don't worry," Lemon said with an evil smile. "You can sue all you want. Well, assuming you survive the being 'touched'." She made air quotes around the word.

Danny turned around to confront me again. "You've got a lot of nerve, bringing thugs to intimidate me." Then he flashed a cocky grin back over his shoulder at the women. "Wouldn't mind gettin' to know the bitches, though."

The second the words were out of his mouth, something settled inside me. I wouldn't have to take care of my brother. Because Rocket was about to.

Except it wasn't Rocket who reached him first. Apple punted him in the back of the knee, causing him to fall. Lemon followed her by giving Danny a motorcycle boot to the head. He wasn't out, but there was no way he was fighting. Or running.

"It's the bitches you gotta worry about. The thugs are basically harmless." Lemon grinned down at Danny. It wasn't a pleasant smile. "Also, if you believe your girlfriend, the mother of your children, was just killed, should you really be thinkin' 'bout gettin' to know the bitches?"

Then Apple delivered another kick to the head. "Do you even know what happened here?"

Danny groaned, clutching his head in his arms. I knelt down next to him, grabbing a handful of his hair and forcing him to look at me.

"They didn't kill Evelyn, you worthless piece of shit. They killed Dad."

Danny's eyes got wide, and he shook his head, mouthing the word "no." I held his gaze, letting my bombshell sink in.

"Dad?"

"That's right. Could just as easily have been one of the kids. They were in the house with him. Bullet rebounded off something and went through the front window. Dad took it in the back."

"That's not possible." He'd gone pale, his eyes wide and wild.

I turned to address Ringo. "You said not here. I ain't lettin' him go. What do you want me to do?" As sergeant at arms, Dom was in charge of security. Ringo was in charge of carrying out Dom's orders.

Ringo turned to Dom, who turned to Rocket. The president put his arm around Lemon, who snuggled against him. Neither of them was ever shy about being affectionate with each other, even in a situation like this.

"Lemon filled me in. Got two choices. Let the authorities deal with it or take him back to the compound. Either way, we'll need some kind of proof."

"Already disturbed the scene," Ringo said. "We packaged Mr. Knoxville for transport to wherever Knox wants to bury him."

"Well, I guess that answers that. Crush and Byte are already looking into Danny's movements since the fire. If he did this, they'll find out." Rocket stepped toward me, reaching out a hand. I took it without hesitation. "I'm sorry for your loss, Knox. Lemon said your father was one hell of a man."

"He was. Thanks to you and Lemon, I got to reconnect with him." I shook my head, emotion clogging my throat. "I missed out on the last fifteen years."

"Your father was so proud of you." Lemon reached out and put her hand over mine and Rocket's. "You got to be with him these last few weeks. You got to introduce me to him. Evelyn and Luke and Aneshya got to have you in their lives. All of them love you, Knox."

I snorted. "Never pegged you as the mushy type, Lemon. I can't wait to tell Falcon. He's gonna eat this shit up."

She scowled, but the corner of her lips tugged up. "I take it back. You are a dumbass."

Rocket chuckled, squeezing my hand tightly once before letting go. "You have a cage and a trailer here?"

"Yes. I used the trailer to move furniture here right after the fire." I shrugged. "I intended to bring everyone back to the compound. I was just trying to get Dad to agree to come with us. His only objection was leaving Danny alone."

"A father is a father," Rocket said. "He knew you could take care of yourself and Evelyn and her kids.

Danny had no one other than your dad."

"Knox?" I turned to see Evelyn standing on the porch just outside the door. "Is everything all right?"

"Yeah, honey. At least, it will be." I climbed the three steps up to the porch and pulled her into my arms. "Would you mind going back inside? I'll have some things to discuss with you and the kids in a minute."

"That's Danny," she said, not answering my question. "Is he dead?" She looked up at me, her eyes wide but not accusing.

"No."

"Why is he on the ground, bleeding?" Again, she didn't sound accusing or suspicious, just curious.

I sighed. I didn't want to tell her what I suspected. The facts were much cleaner. If my suspicions proved right, I'd figure out a way to tell her then. "Honey, I don't know the particulars, but we're gonna find out."

"Don't believe anything these people say, Evie." Danny had shaken off the blows to the head and was now trying to get Evelyn's attention. He yelled his order to her, and Evelyn's gaze found him. "I came here for you. I was afraid you'd been hurt. You might think Denver cares about you, but he doesn't care about anyone. He left us without a backward glance. You don't think he'll do that to you and the kids too? Me and Dad are immediate family. Do you honestly think he'll stay with you when he wouldn't stay with us?"

"Why would you think I'd been hurt?" Evelyn didn't show any emotion, her face blank. I could see the truth in her eyes, though. She knew something was up, she just didn't know what.

"Because there were gunshots. People heard."

"There aren't any neighbors around. No one called the police, or if they did, they didn't show up. It's only been a few minutes since it happened. How'd you know about this so quickly?" Yeah. She was thinking the same thing I was.

"I'm the father of your children. We've been together for thirteen years! That has to count for something."

"I thought it did." Her voice was soft, and I felt her tremble where she leaned into me. "You've been with your wife for fifteen years. At least, that's how long you've been married. I assume you've actually been together longer. Does that mean something to you too?"

"It's over between me and Jordan. I told her I love you and my children."

Evelyn studied him for several seconds, then shook her head. "You're lying, Danny."

"Evelyn." Danny gave her a look like he thought she was confused. "You don't know these people. Not really. We have a long history together. I know we have some issues to work through, but we've been together a long time. You know me."

"Yeah, Danny. I know you. That's the whole problem." Evelyn lifted her head to me. "I trust you, Knox. Whatever you tell me, I'll believe."

"Will you come with me back to the Grim Road compound? It's a secret place, and we'll have to figure out some things for the kids, but we're already working on a system of homeschooling."

"We can't leave?"

"I'll explain it all to you, and I'll admit it's still a fluid situation, but there is a reason Grim Road is secret. The same reason I let my family believe I was dead. You won't be prisoners, but there are some rules you'll need to follow about coming and going. Will you trust me?"

"I trusted your father more than any other person in my life. He made it abundantly clear he wanted you and me together. Whatever I have to do to honor his last wishes, I'll do as long as you promise you'll make sure my kids are safe and have everything they need."

I smiled down at her, leaning in to kiss her, then pressed my forehead to hers. "On my life, Evelyn. On my Goddamned life."

Chapter Ten

Evelyn

My head felt like it was going to explode. At first, I didn't believe what Apple told me. The idea that a man I'd shared a large part of the last thirteen years with, a man I believed I was in a permanent relationship with, a man who had fathered both my children, had just tried to have me killed just didn't compute. But when Danny told me he loved me and the children, I *knew*. It was the same face, the same tone of voice he'd used all these years to deceive me. This man wasn't capable of loving anyone but himself.

"Just a little longer, baby," Knox put an arm around me and guided me inside. Instead of taking me back to my bedroom, though, he took me through the house and around to the backyard. Grover had a small shed where he kept tools. Knox took me straight to the shed and shoved me inside, closing the door behind us.

"OK, honey. Rage all you need to."

It was like a dam broke. Knox's permission to lose my shit broke loose everything I'd been trying to keep inside. Losing Grover had been bad enough, but just the thought of what Danny had done...

"The kids were right there, Knox! They were right fucking there!"

"I know, honey."

"They could have been killed!"

"They weren't, though. They weren't. I'll find out if Danny was involved. If he was, I'll take care of him. He'll never hurt you or the kids again."

I pushed back to look up at Knox, tears streaming from my eyes down my cheeks. I knew I probably looked horrible -- a pretty crier I was not -- but I needed Knox to really pay attention to what I needed to say.

"Whatever happens, I don't want the kids to know." I shook my head violently. "Not about this. It's bad enough what happened. If Danny did something -- anything -- they can never know."

"Honey --"

"No! I mean it, Knox! *They do not know*! Ever!"

"OK, Evelyn. I swear I'll never tell them. But you know Luke is smart enough to figure it out."

"I don't care. I'm not telling them, and I don't want you to, either. If he figures it out and asks --"

"I'm not going to lie to him, Evelyn, and I don't think you will either. He's already in super-protective mode over you and Aneshya. He trusts me right now. If I lie to him, I destroy that trust."

I sobbed then, knowing he was right. Knox pulled me tighter against him and held me for long, long moments. He let me cry and rage. I'm sure I screamed into his chest more than once. Through my entire breakdown, Knox held me. He soothed me with his presence, with his lips in my hair and his arms around me. I'd never had anyone to hold me like this. To encourage me to get out all the emotion I had pent up inside and let me know someone cared about me.

It was all too much. I knew if I didn't find some way to get out all this emotion, I was going to start screaming again. So I took Knox's face in my hands and pulled him down for a kiss. I thrust my tongue into his mouth, needing for him to take control but unable to voice my needs. Knox, being the dominant man I knew he was, immediately swept me up into his arms and set me on a workbench.

He continued to kiss me even as he ran his hands up my shirt to cup my breasts. When he squeezed, I thrust my chest out, wanting more. Needing his touch to be rough and demanding.

"Knox!" I gasped out his name into his mouth.

"You need me." That wasn't a question.

"Yes."

"Do you trust me?" He trailed his mouth from my lips to my ear, then down my neck to my collarbone.

"I do! Please, Knox!"

He stepped back to whip my shirt over my head. Knox wrapped his arms around my torso before fastening his lips around one nipple. I couldn't help the scream, especially when he bit down. Instead of dampening my need, the sharp pain seemed to inflame it. My hands flew to his head, threading through his hair.

Knox growled, and I felt the vibration from my nipple straight to my clit. My cries weren't subtle. On my second scream, Knox clamped a hand over my mouth. Then he was by my ear, whispering.

"That's it, my beautiful little wanton. You're close to coming, aren't you? I haven't even touched your clit." I nodded because he still had his hand over my mouth. "Don't you come until I tell you."

What? How the fuck was I supposed to do that? Especially with Knox biting, suckling, and licking my nipples. The man seemed to know exactly how to bring me up, then let me float back down before I crested the hill.

The more he teased and played with my tits, the more out of control I felt. It was like I was on a roller-coaster, only I couldn't quite get to the top. I knew that once I finally made it to the top of that first hill, the plunge downward would probably drive me mad.

Knox pushed me back, so I rested against the wall while he worked the fastenings of my jeans. He forced them down over my hips, taking my panties with them. The second they were out of the way, Knox dipped his head to swipe his tongue through my folds.

My muffled scream was loud in the little shed. Thank God, Knox put his hand back over my mouth, because I was sure I was loud enough as it was. The very last thing I wanted was for someone to come in on us.

Then Knox smacked the side of my thigh. "Eyes on me, Evelyn," he snapped. "You look at me. Keep your attention on me." He licked me again, and I felt moisture gush from my pussy with each masterful stroke from his tongue.

I did as he commanded because I was helpless to do anything else. Knox was my anchor. He was driving me higher and higher, and I knew that when he finally let me fall, I'd give him everything inside me.

He took a couple more tastes from my cunt before he lifted me and spun me around. Taking my wrists in each hand, he placed them on the bench, pushing my back until I bent at the waist, resting my upper body on the cool wood.

I heard a ripping sound and turned to look over my shoulder as Knox slipped the condom over his cock. He bared his teeth at me before gripping my hair and forcing me to face forward.

"Stay still," he growled at me, his hand holding my back down to keep me in the position he wanted me in.

Then he entered me in one sharp, swift stroke. I sucked in a breath to scream, but Knox's hand clamped over my mouth once more. His hot breath was harsh in my ear, and I shuddered.

Only giving me precious seconds to adjust to his size, Knox started to fuck me. Hard, fast strokes hitting deep inside me put every nerve ending I had on high alert. I felt like I was about to explode out of my skin. It felt good. It felt freeing. Like the buildup swamping me would get rid of all this restless energy. And grief.

I braced my hands on the wooden bench and pushed back, fucking Knox while he fucked me. I needed more. I needed him to take complete control and force me to his will. I think maybe I needed to know he was not only capable of dominating me, but that he would when I needed it.

As if he read my mind, Knox snagged my arms and pulled them back behind me. He looped his arm through them and held my upper arm with one hand while the other clamped back over my mouth once more.

The second he had a good grip, Knox *pounded* inside me. Like a jackhammer. I was completely overloaded. All I could do was take what Knox gave me.

"That's my good girl," he praised. "Takin' my cock so fuckin' good."

I grunted behind his hand, sucking in air through my nose and screaming.

"You need to come?"

I tried to scream that, yes, I need to come so fucking bad, but Knox didn't remove his hand. He seemed to understand, though, because he put his mouth right beside my ear and growled, "Come."

Like he'd flipped a switch inside me, my body detonated. My knees gave out, but Knox held me up. He didn't stop fucking me. Knox pinned my body between his and the bench, his cock as deeply inside me as he could get it. I screamed behind his hand, thrashing in his arms while a raging, angry orgasm engulfed me. The blast was nothing short of nuclear.

Every emotion inside of me seemed to focus on that fucking orgasm, dragging it out to give my body and mind enough time to expel all the negative emotions, the grief in my heart.

When I finally reached the bottom, I was exhausted. I couldn't stand, but that didn't seem to matter. Knox kept an arm clamped around my waist to hold me up as he fixed my pants and snagged my shirt. I floated on a tranquil sea after the storm. Knox was my anchor. My rock. The glue holding me together.

"I love you, Knox." I have no idea where the words came from, but I couldn't deny them, or take them back. I didn't want to do either. For all he'd done for me and given me, Knox deserved to know the truth. And that truth was I was completely in love with the man. Anything I thought I'd felt for Danny was nothing compared to the love I felt for Knox. Nothing.

"I love you too, baby. I'll always take care of you and the kids. I swear I'll be by your side for the rest of my life."

"I need you. I'll always need you."

"I feel the same way. My dad knew what he was doing when he told me to be the man you needed."

"I'll be what you need too. I want to give you the peace you've given me."

"Honey, you already do."

It struck me then how much I'd missed in my life. I had two wonderful kids I loved with all my heart. Yet, I'd never had someone to stand beside me and help me, both with the kids and as a life partner. Danny had been in and out of our lives, but I'd settled for the part of himself he gave us and hadn't asked the hard questions.

"If I'd demanded more from him early on, maybe I'd have prevented it going this far. Christ,

Knox! I lived with the man for thirteen years!"

"It's amazing what you can accept if you live with it long enough, baby. All of this is on Danny. Not you. Never you, Evelyn."

"And poor Luke. Keeping what he saw to himself for *weeks*."

"Luke is smart. And so protective of you and Aneshya. He's a great kid. Gonna be an even better man."

Knox was breaking my heart. Had I ever heard Danny praise Luke like that? Even if Luke wasn't physically here, it was still more than Danny had ever said to or about the boy.

"That's all because of you, honey. You taught him right from wrong and how you treat family. You. Not Danny."

She sniffed, scrubbing the back of her wrist under her nose. "Your dad did too. No matter how often Danny was gone, your father was always there."

"Dad was like that."

"My parents were older when they had me. Mom was forty-two and Dad was forty-seven. Both of them died in their late sixties, so the kids were pretty young. They were too young to remember them, so they didn't get a lot of quality time together. They knew Mom and Dad loved them, but it was your dad who passed on the life lessons fathers should pass on to their kids."

"It was obvious how much he loved them."

"It was." I broke down again, crying into Knox's chest while he held me. We stood in that shed, and he let me cry, never once trying to hush me. He understood my need to grieve. I was sure he was doing his own grieving. "You just got your dad back only to lose him."

"Yes. But I got to make things right with him.

Got to show him how much he meant to me. He might not have liked that I left without telling him why or where I was going, but Dad was a Marine. He understood sometimes things don't go the way they're supposed to."

"Is that what happened?" I looked up at him. Knox had said he was going to take care of us, that he was going to take us to his club's compound, but I needed to know what that meant. I'd still go no matter what, though. Because no matter how short a time I'd had with Knox, I knew I never wanted to be without him. Not so long as my kids had what they needed.

"Yeah, in a nutshell. I can't tell you everything because it's classified, but I can tell you that some of the things I've done for my country would get me killed."

"So it was dangerous."

"Still is. That's why we have our own hidden little sanctuary. It's self-sustaining for the most part, so we don't have to leave if we don't want to. It's only been recently we've started getting out more."

"Is everyone in Grim Road like you?"

"You mean are they Black Ops? Yeah. Every single one of us has worked on unsanctioned missions for the government. Usually the CIA."

"I guess I'm a little naive, but I thought that kind of thing only existed in the movies."

"It's not something anyone really talks about. The movies make it a little more glamorous than it really is, but the bottom line is, when the lines of legality and sometimes morality get blurred." He snorted. "Or obliterated entirely. When that happens, if it's time for an election and a possible administration change, you try to put everything on hold until you know who's gonna be in charge. What could earn you a medal with one president could send you to prison with another."

"I never thought about it that way."

"And I never want you to have to again. I disappeared not only because of what I did, but because of what I know. My handler on my last mission didn't expect me to make it home alive. It was a suicide mission."

"Knox! Oh, God!"

"Fortunately for me, I didn't get the memo. Got in and out with barely a scratch. When I couldn't reach anyone at the pick-up point, I broke protocol and called Rocket. He was my team leader. He directed me to a secondary pick-up point and sent his own people after me. That's when I joined Grim Road. The club's been around since before the formation of the CIA, but most of us are there now because of our ties to that agency."

"So that's why you keep to yourselves."

"Yes. We've come out of our compound and into the city more in the last few months than we have in all the years since I've been there, but we still have to be careful. We'll always have to look over our shoulders and keep our heads down, but with the proper paperwork for the vehicles and bikes, as well as some creative identity manufacturing, we manage."

"You said you were working on homeschooling for the kids?"

"Yeah. Effie is living with Rocket and Lemon. She's not much younger than Aneshya. Gina and Lemon are getting a homeschooling program together for her. I see no reason Luke and Aneshya can't do the same. If they need more help than what we can give them here, we'll figure something else out. There's a club in Kentucky called Bones MC. We have ties to them through our weapons guy and a couple named Mama and Pops. Their president's old lady is a teacher. If we need to, we'll contact Cain for help."

"Are you sure we won't be in the way? I don't want to be a bother."

"Honey, it doesn't matter if you're in the way. You're coming with me. You gave me your trust, and I'm not lettin' you take it back. I want you with me. I want the kids with me. I'll do whatever I need to make you comfortable in order for all of you to be with me."

I took a breath. Looking up into Knox's eyes, I could see not only the sincerity but the determination to make that happen. This was a man who wanted us where Danny never had. It felt like something settling in my chest. An easing of pressure and stress. "OK." It was all I could manage around the lump in my throat.

"Good. Leave it all to me. All you have to do is what I tell you. If you have questions, ask. But I swear I'll do right by all of you."

The thing was, I believed him. With all my heart, I believed him.

Chapter Eleven

Knox

We pulled into the compound in late afternoon. Evelyn hadn't said much and the kids were pretty quiet. Aneshya was taking Dad's death pretty hard. Luke was occupying his mind by fussing over Evelyn and Aneshya, but he was having trouble as well. Evelyn was just shell-shocked. They'd all been through so much I was surprised she'd only had the one meltdown. Thankfully, she seemed better than in those first few minutes and, most importantly, she hadn't fallen back into that despair.

As we pulled through the gate, a couple of men pulled in front of us as an escort. That told me there was news, likely that the club had found the shooter and had him on club grounds. I'd follow our escorts and let them guide us where Rocket wanted us. I'd learn what they'd found then.

Not surprisingly, they had us go straight to the family area. Our compound was completely fenced off with the common areas around the outside. The club whores and our family areas were both fenced off inside the main compound giving both areas an extra layer of protection. The whole thing was over a square mile with our territory inside the wildlife sanctuary extending a much larger area. As a result, we were able to keep the overgrowth thick to prevent us being spotted from the air.

As we entered the family compound, I followed the escort until they pulled into the driveway of one of the larger cabins we'd built. It would be large enough for us all to be comfortable and for the kids to each have their own room.

I shut off the truck, then turned to Evelyn and

the kids. "I think this is where we're gonna set up shop. You guys wanna take a look around?"

Aneshya sniffed but nodded her head. Luke took his sister's hand and squeezed. She smiled at him, and I thought that maybe they'd be all right.

Once out of the truck, I helped Aneshya out, then went around to Evelyn's side. She'd just slid from the truck when I reached her. She stepped into my arms willingly without hesitation, and I hugged her close.

"Hey, guys." Falcon approached us, a welcoming smile on his face. "Lemon said you were coming to stay with us." He held out a hand to Luke. "I'm Falcon." Luke took his hand and nodded at him.

"I'm Luke. This is my sister, Aneshya."

The girl gave Falcon a shy smile but didn't say anything. She clung to her brother, and Luke put an arm around her.

"It's good to meet you, Aneshya. You know Lemon and Apple, right?"

"Yeah," Luke answered. "We like them."

"Good. They're waiting in the house. Thought you'd like to explore and pick out your rooms." Falcon continued to smile but gave me a look. "You think you can do that while your mom and Knox go see Rocket? Me and Bear over there'll be outside if you guys need us."

"Mommy?" Aneshya looked up at Evelyn. I wasn't sure if the girl was afraid or if she was asking permission, but Evelyn knew her daughter.

She knelt down in front of the girl. "I promise I'll be back as soon as I can. I doubt Rocket will keep us too long. No one's gonna hurt you or Luke."

"You're gonna protect us now?" Aneshya addressed me, her eyes wide and questioning.

"I sure am. Me and everyone here. We're all one

big family."

That seemed to please Aneshya because she finally had a real, if small, smile. "I like that."

"We're learning how important it is to have family you can rely on, so we like it too."

Evelyn lifted her face to me, giving me a questioning look. I nodded. "Stay with Lemon and Apple. I'll be right back."

Luke stepped up to me. "You take care of my mom. I'll protect Aneshya."

"On my word, Luke. Your mother will be safe. So will you and Aneshya."

Luke and I shared a long look, then Luke nodded. "I don't think you're like Danny. You're his brother, but you're not like him."

"I won't betray any of you, Luke. Not for anything. Do you understand?"

"Yeah. I do." Luke stuck out his hand to me and I took it. He gave me a firm handshake. "If you do to Mom what Danny did, I'll kill you."

"I expect nothing less. You've got more of your grandpa in you than your father."

That seemed to please Luke because he lifted his chin and I saw the ghost of a smile and something like shock. Like I'd just given the kid the highest praise. He nodded once, then took his sister's hand and led her toward the house. We watched until they opened the door. Apple and Lemon greeted them with smiles and hugs. To my amusement, Luke hugged Apple for a very long time. Before Apple finally pushed him off, she was laughing, and Luke was smiling. Then Apple rolled her eyes, threw up her hands, and hugged him again. Luke had a shit-eating grin on his face. I knew one day he'd be capable of breaking hearts wherever he went. The thing was, because of the way Danny had lied to his family, by deceiving them all, Luke would never intentionally harm a woman or child. Physically, mentally, or emotionally. As I saw it, my job now was to reinforce those instincts in him by proving I would always love and protect his family now.

My family.

With that last, though, I leaned in and kissed Evelyn's cheek. "Come on. Let's go see what's going on so we can get back and make sure everyone gets settled in."

Evelyn nodded, then turned her face up to mine. She pulled herself up on her tiptoes and kissed my mouth tenderly. I wrapped my arms around her, kissing her back.

"You up for this? I can go by myself if you want to stay with your kids."

"No. I need to know what happened. And why."

"I know. But you know I can explain it all. After." I wanted to spare her what I knew would be a painful encounter but knew she wouldn't take me up on the offer.

"No. I need to see the truth in his eyes."

"He's lied to you before, Evelyn."

"I know, Knox."

She tried to look away, but I turned her face gently back to me. "I'm not criticizing you, honey. I just don't want to cause you more pain that you've already endured."

"I know. But I need to do this. I'll trust you to have my back."

"You'll do what I tell you? I promised your son I'd never hurt you. If someone else hurts you on my watch, that kid'll jack me in my sleep." I grinned down at her, trying to lighten the mood while still getting her promise to do what I said. If Rocket found out something to condemn Danny and he managed to tug at Evelyn's heart strings, I might not be able to keep that promise to Luke. And I had no desire to, and no intention of, breaking that promise.

She smiled back, though it didn't really reach her eyes. "Yes, Mr. Bossy Pants. I promise I'll do what you tell me. I wouldn't want my son to have to hurt you."

"Good. 'Cause if I get my ass handed to me by a twelve-year-old, Lemon will take my man card." As I hoped, that got a small giggle from her. "Well, it isn't much, but I'll take it." I smiled down at her, relieved that maybe I could see this through without hurting Evelyn any more than she'd already been.

"I love you, Knox," she whispered. "You're a good man. Don't let anyone tell you differently."

"If anyone else hears that, it'll ruin my reputation." I grinned. "But you're the only one who really matters. You and Luke and Aneshya."

"Let's get this over with. I want to move on with my life. And I want you in it."

"That's my girl." I pulled her close and kissed the top of her head.

We got back in the truck, and I drove deeper into the fenced area of our territory. I knew where Rocket was with Danny. I didn't dread this as much as I simply wanted it to be over. What I wanted to know was why. Why all of it. Why hadn't he left his wife? Why hadn't he told Evelyn about the other woman? Why had he not changed something when Evelyn became pregnant? Why had he let it all continue and built a separate life with Evelyn when he already had a woman he obviously didn't want to leave?

If he'd had something to do with the attack at the house, why had he done it? And yeah, that possibility was something I couldn't let go of. In my heart, I was sure he at least knew about it. But was it him or his wife? Or someone his wife knew, like her father or brother or *anyone* other than Danny. Because if he'd had no idea it was going to happen, he might get to live. If he'd had anything to do with it or knew it was happening and did nothing about it? Yeah. He wouldn't survive the night.

Grim Road had a two-room, partially underground building constructed into a large knoll. We used it for storage, but in cases like this, it doubled as an interrogation room. There was already a gathering of officers outside who needed to preside and offer judgment recommendations. Rocket had the final say, but this was a serious gathering of members outside of church.

Rocket and Dom leaned against the door talking, while Spike, Leather, and Mace strolled in our direction to greet us as we got out of the truck. Evelyn had slid to my side, because she'd folded up the console and sat next to me in the middle of the front seat. She hadn't spoken during the short ride, but had gripped my arm and laid her face against my shoulder.

I helped her down just as the trio reached us. Evelyn had met nearly everyone in Grim Road over the weeks since the fire. She'd made an impression with them all as a kind woman and a wonderful mother. I was proud to have her for my old lady.

Mace gave Evelyn a warm smile. "Though I'm glad to see you, Evelyn, I didn't think you'd want to come to this. You know, you already told Lemon what happened from your perspective. You don't have to be here."

"I know," Evelyn whispered. "I need to see this through, though. I want some answers, and Danny is the only one who can give them to me."

"You can tell us," Leather coaxed. "We'll get you any answers you need. You won't have to be anywhere around him."

Evelyn shook her head. "No. This is something I need to do. I lived with him for thirteen years. I want to look into his eyes when he's questioned. See the truth for myself."

"I know you don't want to hear this," Mace continued, "and understand I mean no disrespect, but you didn't know he'd been lying to you all that time. Are you sure you can tell when he's lying now?"

Evelyn gave a small smile. "I know I can, now. I think I always could, I just chose to ignore my gut." She shook her head slightly. "I didn't want to admit to myself he had another woman, but I think I knew the whole time. What I didn't know was that I was the other woman. Not her."

Yeah. Danny was a dead man. I could see how this hurt Evelyn. How embarrassed she was. Humiliated. Even if he had nothing to do with the shooting at our old house, I'd probably beat Danny to a fucking bloody pulp on principle.

"I'm sorry he put you through this, Evelyn." Mace held out his hand for Evelyn to take. "You're a good woman. I'm glad Knox found you."

That seemed to take Evelyn by surprise. She gave him a startled look, then the ghost of a smile formed on her lips. "Thank you. I appreciate you saying so." She took his hand and shook it firmly. "I'm so glad he has this club. I love the way you have each other's backs." She looked up at me, and her smile seemed more relaxed as she did. "Everyone needs someone."

"I have you too, baby. But yeah. You can thank Lemon later. She's the one who taught us we needed to open up and share more with each other so we *could* have each other's backs."

"I'll most definitely do that."

"You guys ready?" Leather looked from me to Evelyn and back.

Evelyn lifted her chin and put her shoulders back. Her hand found mine and held it tightly. "I am."

I smiled at my brave little warrior. She might not be a fighter so much as a protector, but she would absolutely do whatever she had to do for her children. And I was certain she was doing this for them as much as herself, especially since I was pretty sure she knew Danny would die tonight. She needed to have something to tell her children when it was all over.

"Let's do this."

Chapter Twelve

Evelyn

I'd never been so nervous in my life. Not only did I have to face Danny in a room full of… not exactly strangers, but men I was embarrassed to look so stupid in front of. These men were Knox's family. If he truly meant to keep me in his life like I intended to keep him, then they would soon be my family too. Lemon and Apple already felt like younger sisters.

We walked into the bunker. There was a half staircase leading down where they'd dug into and slightly underneath the small knoll to hide this place but left enough room to work in. One side was filled with what looked like stored boxes and canned goods, while the other side held a table, chairs, and various instruments that might have been torture devices. Might have been tools. I had no idea what they were used for, but it was questionable. The point was, Danny was eyeing them nervously. I didn't blame him. He was tied to the chair he was sitting in. It was obvious he wasn't here to have a pleasant chat.

Two men were already inside talking to Danny. I'd met them both when Knox moved things into the house. Piston and Rattler turned to look at us as we stepped inside the small room.

"Y'all ready for this?" Rattler's smile was pure evil. Like he was going to enjoy whatever happened next and made no apologies for it.

Piston sat in a chair he'd turned around so he straddled the seat and rested his forearms on the back. Rattler leaned against the wall next to the table where the tools had been laid out in a neat row.

"Knox." Danny looked scared as I'd ever seen him. He usually had a cunning look about him I'd misread in the past as him being absorbed in thought about his work. I guess he'd had to be cunning to juggle two women living in the same fucking apartment building.

Knox and Rocket exchanged a look until Rocket nodded. Permission for Knox to start? "Who told you Evelyn had been shot?"

"One of the neighbors. He heard the gunshots and --"

"Cut the shit, Danny! There were no neighbors. No one noticed enough to call the cops. No one but those of us near the house knew. So I'm asking you one more time. Who told you?"

"I can get it out of him if you want, Knox." Rattler picked up a small saw blade, looking it over like the cheesy villain in a movie. "We can start with his toes and work our way up."

"What the fuck? Knox! *What the fuck*?" Danny was panting now, looking from the small saw to Knox and back, not wanting to take his eyes off the threat. Then he turned his gaze on me. "Evie! Tell them I'd never hurt you. You know I wouldn't."

I had to literally bite my tongue to keep silent. At one time in my life, I might have solidly backed him up. Not now, though. He was a master at manipulating me. I'd chosen to let him by ignoring warning signs. Despite the fact he was the father of my children, despite the fact that my instinct was to support him, I absolutely would not take his side in this. These men would get the truth out of him because Knox said they would. I believed Knox because I'd trusted his father more than anyone else in my life, and he'd trusted Knox.

"Tell me what I want to know," Knox insisted.

Danny shook his head. Knox stepped forward

and punched him in the nose. Blood squished between his face and Knox's knuckles, and Danny squealed like a pig, trying to get up from the chair but unable to because of his bonds. He probably thought he could run away, but that obviously wasn't happening.

"No one else was supposed to get hurt." His expression crumpled, and Danny started crying. "No one else, I swear."

"Why Evelyn?" It was a demand, not a question. When Danny just started sobbing, Knox repeated himself. "Why. Evelyn." There was an edge of violence about Knox I'd never seen before. It was like he was struggling to suppress his anger but was now losing the battle.

"Because Jordan won't take me back!" Danny yelled his answer, his gaze darting to mine. I saw resentment there. Frustration maybe? I didn't know. Didn't much care. "She said she couldn't live with knowing I had another woman out there I had a family with when she'd struggled to have children of her own."

"How would killing Evelyn fix that problem? Sounds like your wife is done with you, no matter what."

"If I had custody of the kids and Evelyn was gone, she'd let me come back. She'd have the children we always wanted, and everything could go back to the way it was!"

If he'd slapped me, I wasn't sure I'd have been more surprised. "She actually told you that?" I knew I should have kept my mouth shut, but I couldn't seem to. The question slipped out. Had I been living in the shadow of not one, but two sociopaths?

"She didn't have to," he spat at me, his anger turned fully in my direction now. "She wanted kids.

She lost the one she was carrying after the fire. She'd be happy to have my children, no matter how old they are."

"And if she didn't, Danny? What if she wanted babies instead of older kids -- children who would have reminded her every day that you'd led a double life -- one of those lives without her. What if she rejected you then?"

"She wouldn't," Danny said, confidence ringing in his voice even as tears still streamed down his face.

"I didn't ask if she *would*, Danny. I asked what would have happened if she did. What would you have done if you'd killed me and Jordan didn't want Luke and Aneshya and refused to take you back?"

Danny looked away and I had my answer.

"Got any idea how a blood brother of mine has turned out so Goddamned dumb?" Knox addressed the question to Rocket who shrugged.

"Not sure. I mean, Lemon said you never struck her as particularly bright. Until you claimed Evelyn, that is." He grinned. "I think she'd agree you're not a dumbass. Your brother, on the other hand? Yeah. Did either of your parents smoke? Maybe it was a birth defect?"

Knox snorted. "You've been hangin' with the VP too long, prez."

Rocket scowled. "Christ. That *is* something she'd say, innit." Rocket shook his head before addressing Danny. "You admit you're the one who killed Grover Knoxville in an attempt to kill Evelyn?"

"I didn't kill anybody!"

"But you had someone else do it."

"How do you know it was me? It could have been Jordan." Danny gave a nervous laugh. "I'm broke! I don't have a job. *Never* had a job! Jordan is the one with all the money. Her and her parents."

There was movement at the door. I started and moved my hand from Knox's to his arm, gripping tightly and moving so that I was sheltered in the strength of his body. I knew I was safe here, or thought I was, but I was so off-balance I wasn't sure I could hold it together much longer.

Crush stepped inside and shut the door behind him. He met my gaze and ducked his head. "Sorry, Evelyn. Didn't mean to startle you."

"It's OK." My voice was barely above a whisper. "Not your fault."

He patted me on the shoulder awkwardly before tossing a file on the table where Piston sat. Rocket picked it up and thumbed through it, his face hard and unreadable.

"You confirmed all this." It wasn't a question.

"Everything. Byte did the initial research. I corroborated everything he dug up."

Rocket tossed the folder back on the table and scrubbed a hand over his face. "Did you find the shooters?"

"Yep. Ringo took care of them. He's currently spreading them over the Everglades region outside our territory. Different… regions." Crush looked very uncomfortable as he glanced back-and-forth from me to Danny.

"Good. Knox? There anything else you need to know before we take care of this?"

Knox looked down at me. I shook my head, blinking back tears. "He's insane," I whispered.

"He's a megalomaniac," Crush said. "He was in it for the power and the money." He shook his head slightly. "Power from being able to keep you and the kids on the line without his wife knowing. Money from his wife and her family. He'd been slowly siphoning off funds from a variety of his wife's accounts. Looked like he'd recently gotten into some of her father's accounts as well. If things had gone on the way they had been, I have no doubt he'd have cleaned them both out eventually."

"That's not true, Evie," Danny jumped in. It was easy to see the sweat on his face. "You know me."

"Yeah, Danny." I sighed, shaking my head. "I know you. And you're lying. You did all of that. And tried to have me killed. You'd have killed your own children to further whatever scheme you were playing at." I thought I'd have some kind of breakdown, but I felt strangely at peace. I'd weathered what could have been the worst thing to happen in my life outside of my parents' death. Grover hadn't tried to replace my father in my life, but I came to think of him as an extension of my father. They'd have liked each other. "I have no idea what's going to happen to you, but I'm sure it won't be pleasant."

"Damned straight," Knox muttered. He pulled me into his arms, and I let him. Right now, there was no other place I wanted to be than with Knox.

"You want me to have Lemon come get her?" Rocket spoke softly.

"Evie! What about the kids? They need their father!"

"You lost the right to call them that when you had someone try to kill me with the kids nearby." I jerked, shoving away from Knox and moving closer to Danny. "You tried to kill me, Danny. With Luke and Aneshya *right there*." My voice shook. Hell, my whole body trembled.

"Yeah, Evie, I heard you the first time," he muttered. That was the Danny I knew. The one who talked down to me when he got drunk or was generally frustrated. It didn't happen often, but when it did, I wanted to make him hurt the way he'd made me hurt. I thought that, now, maybe I could dish out what I should have years ago.

"You did, huh?" I wanted to hit him. To hurt him like he'd hurt Grover. Unfortunately, not only did I not have something to hit him with, I wasn't that kind of person. I didn't have it in me to really hurt someone unless it was in defense of my kids. It was the thought that they could have been hurt that brought me to this state of mind in the first place, but they were home safe with Lemon, Apple, and three of Grim Road's men protecting them. So I did the only thing I could do. I spat in Danny's face. "Did you hear that? No? That's the sound of how many fucks I give about you. You disgust me!"

"Evelyn. Evie." Danny gave me his best pleading face. "You know they're gonna kill me unless you do something."

"I'm not sure I could do anything to change the outcome for you even if I wanted to." A hand rested on my shoulder gently. Without even looking I knew it was Knox. "You dug your own grave. Now, it's time you lie in it."

"Come on, Evie!"

I turned and buried my face in Knox's chest. "I want to go home."

"Then that's where I'll take you."

"Evie? Please." Danny actually sounded like he was going to cry. "You and the kids are all I've got left!"

I took a deep breath and turned back to him. "Goodbye, Danny."

Chapter Thirteen

Knox

There was nothing in this world I wanted to do more than to see to Danny's demise myself... except take care of Evelyn. She said she wanted to go home, so that's where I was going to take her.

The second she told Danny goodbye I scooped her up and carried her out of the bunker. Rocket and Dom would do what needed to be done and let me know once it was all over.

I carried Evelyn to the truck and set her down beside it. "You gonna be all right?"

She looked up at me. Her eyes were shiny like she was struggling not to cry, but she nodded. "Yes." She took a breath before leaning her head against my chest. "I'm not upset about Danny. Not really. At least, not for me. I think I knew there was nothing between us for a long time. There was a time when I might even have missed him. Maybe on some level I will." She shook her head. "I think it's more I'll miss the man I thought he was."

"You understand this has to be done. Right?"

"Of course." She put her hand on my face and stood up on her tiptoes to brush a kiss on my cheek. "I only wish I was strong enough to do it myself, but I'm not."

"You'll never do anything violent as long as you have me, Evelyn. That's what I'm here for."

"To destroy my problems?"

I chuckled. "You got that right, honey. I get to destroy all your problems."

"You know you can't do that. Right?"

"I can and I will, baby."

Evelyn's lower lip trembled, then with a cry, she threw herself into my arms. I held her tightly while she cried, trying to soothe her but knowing this was probably cathartic for her.

I gave her a few minutes to get herself under control before helping her into the truck. I knew the guys wouldn't do anything until they heard us leave. I really didn't want Evelyn to be here when they killed Danny. It would likely be a clean bullet to the head, but she didn't need to hear or be here when they disposed of his body.

Once we were settled inside the truck, I started it and left the area, moving back to the main section of our territory. I stopped just before we made it in sight of the walled-off family area and put the truck in park.

I shoved my seat back and reached for Evelyn where she sat next to me. "Come here, honey." She didn't resist as I urged her to straddle my lap. I wrapped my arms around her while she let her tears fall. I rubbed her back, not trying to quiet her, but hoping my touch could somehow help her release the emotions I knew she held back.

"Come on, baby. Let it out."

She sucked in a shuddering breath before raising her head to find my lips with hers. She kissed me until I took over, thrusting my tongue deep. Evelyn shuddered in my arms, her fingers digging into my shoulders.

"Need you, Knox." Her whispered plea was the sweetest music. "Please."

I shoved her shirt over her breasts to grip and knead them. She groaned and arched her back, giving me leave to do what I wanted.

"I've got you, baby. I'll always have you."

"Fuck me, Knox. Please. I need…"

"I know. I've got you."

I shoved her bra over her tits and latched on to one nipple with my mouth while I tweaked the other with my fingers. My arm was looped around her back, supporting her while I did my best to take her somewhere wonderful to combat the darkness we'd just come from.

When she struggled to get her jeans down her thighs in the truck, I shoved open the door and pulled her out with me. She tugged me back down to kiss her while I shoved her pants down. Then I spun her around and wrapped her up tightly in my arms.

"I'm gonna fuck you right here, Evelyn. I'm gonna do it bare."

"Please. That's what I want."

I unfastened my pants and pulled my dick out with one hand. Without giving her time to change her mind or confirm that was what she truly wanted, I guided my cock to her entrance and slid inside in a slow, smooth thrust.

It was heaven.

I held myself deep for several seconds until Evelyn's keening cries and the bucking of her hips made it impossible to keep still. With both arms holding her tightly, pinning her arms against her body, I fucked her. Evelyn let me have her, her head falling back to rest just below my shoulder. Her breath exploded from her in little pants forced out by the slamming of my body against hers. With every thrust, she cried out. Her pussy gripped my cock relentlessly, clamping down occasionally when she shivered in pleasure.

"Please, Knox." Her whispered plea sounded as desperate as I felt. I needed to come. To fill her full and stake my final claim on her.

"You want my cum, baby?"

"Yes! So much!"

"Then take it!" I hissed the command in her ear as I slid my hand to her mound and found her clit with my fingers. The second I touched her, she went off. Her cunt squeezed my dick with relentless force. I pulled out, then shoved myself in one last time. Cum erupted from my cock the second I was inside her as far as I could go. I groaned as she screamed, the orgasm we both rode out seeming to ebb and flow in unison.

When she was finally limp in my arms, and I thought my knees would collapse, I let my cock slide from her so I could put her clothing to rights. She'd need to clean up and change once we got back home, but that was a minor thing considering the moment.

"Are you OK?" I nuzzled the side of her neck as I pulled her bra back into place and tugged her shirt down.

"Yes. I am now." She turned in my arms, sliding hers around my neck. "Thank you, Knox. For dragging me out of that fire. For keeping my kids safe. For having such a wonderful dad. For being with me. For everything."

"You never have to thank me, Evelyn. You're my woman, and it's my Goddamned privilege to be your man."

We held each other for a long time before she was ready to go. When she was, I helped her inside the truck before climbing in behind her and starting it up.

"You ready to see Luke and Aneshya?" I wasn't sure what she planned on telling them, but I'd back her up. No matter what.

"Yes. Knox?"

"Yeah, baby."

"I think I'll wait to tell them what happened. I'm not sure I'm ready."

"Up to you. I've got your back whenever you're ready."

"I'm not sure how Aneshya will take it. But it's Luke I'm really worried about."

"He's a strong lad. Give him credit."

"I know he was angry with Danny, but there was a time when they had a good relationship."

"We'll figure it out. I'll be right there with you."

She looked up at me and smiled before wrapping her arms around mine and leaning her head against my shoulder. "I know."

As we took off, I kissed the top of her head. "Love you, Evelyn. I hope you know that."

She rubbed her face against my shoulder. "I love you too."

For the first time since I'd had to leave my old life behind, I felt a peace settle over me. It was like I'd found a place I truly belonged. Sure, Grim Road was my family, but Evelyn was now my world. Her and her kids. I'd protect all of them with my dying breath. This was my home. Evelyn. Wherever she was. I had no idea what the rest of my life had in store for me, but I knew Evelyn would be there with me to enjoy it.

Marteeka Karland

International bestselling author Marteeka Karland leads a double life as an action romance writer by evening and a semi-domesticated housewife by day. Known for her down-and-dirty MC romances, Marteeka takes pleasure in spinning tales of tenacious, protective heroes and spirited heroines. She staunchly advocates that every character deserves a blissful ending.

Marteeka finds joy in baking, and gardening with her husband. Make sure to visit her website to stay updated with her most recent projects. Don't forget to register for her newsletter which will pepper you with a potpourri of Teeka's beloved recipes, book suggestions, autograph events, and a plethora of interesting tidbits.

Marteeka at Changeling: changelingpress.com/marteeka-karland-a-39

Wanda Violet O. (Teeka's Dark Erotica side): changelingpress.com/wanda-violet-o-a-226

Bones MC Multiverse

Bones MC
Shadow Demons
Salvation's Bane MC
Black Reign MC
Iron Tzars MC
Grim Road MC
Bones MC Legends
Bones MC Audio
Salvation's Bane MC Audio
Iron Tzars MC Audio
Grim Road MC Audio
Bones MC Print Duets

Changeling Press LLC

Contemporary Action Adventure, Sci-Fi, Steampunk, Dark Fantasy, Urban Fantasy, Paranormal, and BDSM Romance available in e-book, audio, and print format at ChangelingPress.com -- MC Romance, Werewolves, Vampires, Dragons, Shapeshifters and Horror -- Tales from the edge of your imagination.

Where can I get Changeling Press Books?

Changeling Press e-books are available at ChangelingPress.com, Amazon, Apple Books, Barnes & Noble, Kobo, Smashwords, and other online retailers, including Everand Subscription and Kobo Subscription Services. Print books are available at Amazon, Barnes and Noble, and by ISBN special order through your local bookstores.

Changeling Press, LLC

ChangelingPress.com